KU-742-105

The Rattletrap Trip

Other books by Rachel Anderson

The Poacher's Son
The War Orphan
French Lessons
The Bus People
Paper Faces
When Mum Went to Work
The Working Class
Black Water
The Doll's House
The Scavenger's Tale
Warlands

For young readers

Little Angel Comes to Stay
Little Angel, Bonjour
Happy Christmas, Little Angel

Oxford Myths and Legends

Renard the Fox

The Rattletrap Trip

Rachel Anderson

OXFORD
UNIVERSITY PRESS

OXFORD
UNIVERSITY PRESS

Great Clarendon Street, Oxford OX2 6DP

Oxford University Press is a department of the University of Oxford.
It furthers the University's objective of excellence in research, scholarship,
and education by publishing worldwide in

Oxford New York
Auckland Bangkok Buenos Aires
Cape Town Chennai Dar es Salaam Delhi Hong Kong Istanbul
Karachi Kolkata Kuala Lumpur Madrid Melbourne Mexico City Mumbai
Nairobi São Paulo Shanghai Taipei Tokyo Toronto

Oxford is a registered trade mark of Oxford University Press
in the UK and in certain other countries

Copyright © Rachel Anderson 2003

The moral rights of the author have been asserted

Database right Oxford University Press (maker)

First published 2003

All rights reserved. No part of this publication may be reproduced,
stored in a retrieval system, or transmitted, in any form or by any means,
without the prior permission in writing of Oxford University Press.
Within the UK, exceptions are allowed in respect of any fair
dealing for the purpose of research or private study, or criticism or
review, as permitted under the Copyright, Designs and Patents Act 1988,
or in the case of reprographic reproduction in accordance with
the terms of the licences issued by the Copyright Licensing Agency.
Enquiries concerning reproduction outside these terms and in other
countries should be sent to the Rights Department, Oxford University Press,
at the above address.

This book is sold subject to the condition that it shall not, by way of trade or
otherwise, be lent, re-sold, hired out or otherwise circulated without
the publisher's prior consent in any form of binding or cover other than that in
which it is published and without a similar condition including this condition
being imposed on the subsequent purchaser.

British Library Cataloguing in Publication Data available

ISBN 0 19 271872 X

1 3 5 7 9 10 8 6 4 2

Typeset by AFS Image Setters Ltd, Glasgow

Printed in Great Britain by
Cox & Wyman Ltd, Reading, Berkshire

We Are Sisters

You shouldn't have favourites about people, only about sweeties or pizza toppings or stories, so my mum's mum used to say. Nonetheless, if I did secretly have a favourite, it was Elizabeth. She was sixteen, the eldest of us. Not that she knew it. She couldn't even count up to half, let alone to one. No wonder she couldn't get her shoes on the right feet. She didn't even know she had two feet.

She'd stopped going to school months before this story begins. Sarsaparilla said they treated her disrespectfully and it wasn't doing her any good.

'School isn't doing me any good either,' I said. But I still had to go.

'It's the law,' said Sarsaparilla. 'If you don't go to school, I'll have to go to prison.'

Some people called Elizabeth profoundly disabled, her sweet and darling mind enclosed as it was inside its double-wrap. I preferred to think of her as a holy mystic. Gentle as a cloud, quiet as a whisper, with tiny peering

1

eyes and a broad smile that could fill a whole room with optimism.

Georgie said that if you looked carefully you could actually see the joy radiating outwards from Elizabeth's body.

'Just like it does with our Saviour.'

'How d'you know? Have you ever actually seen him?'

'Not exactly. But I've seen those cards that Sarsaparilla's mum used to bring us. He's radiating those brass rods out of his ever-loving heart, so divinely strong they can reach people in every corner of the world. Even the wretched sinners of the earth who're in hiding.'

Georgie was the nearest to me in age. I wanted to believe all this stuff about burning rods because I wanted to be the same as her and I wanted her to love me. She had thick curly hair sticking out all round like a dark angel's halo. Her skin was the colour of medium-toasted bread and she was as warm and comforting as buttered toast on a rainy afternoon.

Georgie was more powerfully influenced than I by the luridly coloured prayer-cards which showed Jesus in a sky-blue bathrobe, the chest cavity opening like a kitchen cupboard and the incredible organ housed inside like a gold and vermilion honey pot.

'Can't say I approve of what my daughter's doing with you lot,' Sarsaparilla's mum used to say. 'Gathering you all up like this. Still, I don't believe it's just for the money. I'm pretty sure she's got the very best intention at heart.'

I remember asking, 'What's the very best intention?' I needed to know so I could do it too. Back then, I wanted to be totally good, entirely loving, all the time, even if I couldn't quite accept the radiating rods.

'Oh, it'll be love, dearie, it'll always be love. Though different people interpret it in many different ways.'

I missed Sarsaparilla's mum when she died. She was the nearest I ever had to a real nan.

Our Mum and the Unwanted Van

Sarsaparilla collected things. You name it, she had to have it. A rake without a handle. Five empty picture-frames. A grapefruit past its prime.

If ever she saw something which nobody else cared about, then she'd start wanting it. And the more nobody else wanted it, the more determined she was to have it. She'd even pay for things that other people were chucking out.

'When there's life, there's still hope, my petkins,' she'd say.

My brother said it was compulsive and sad, specially when he had to wear the unmatching second-hand socks she'd collected from a church hall sale.

One Thursday evening, she spotted the old camper-van in Mr Singh's front garden further down the street. It was lollipop pink with curly Indian script painted on the side. It had rust spots like orange acne, and a roof-rack that looked sturdy enough to carry an elephant. Mr Singh's Punjabi writing and the roof-rack were clearly the only reliable things about that van.

It was still there on Saturday morning. By Sunday afternoon, Sarsaparilla had entered into a neighbourly conversation with Mr Singh. By Monday, the chat had turned towards negotiation. By Monday evening, the van was hers. Sold for a song to the large lady in the bright flowery dress.

'The poor gorgeous old rattletrap,' Sarsaparilla said. 'Fancy saying she's unroadworthy, just because she's failed that silly old Ministry of Transport test. But with a bit of love and imagination, I'm sure we can coax her through. It'd be a crime to dump her. Let's give her a second chance.' That was what she said about everything she rescued. She was the nation's keenest recycler.

Sarsaparilla had never owned a vehicle before. She had a bike. But we'd never seen her on it. Perhaps it was because she was too fat to balance safely.

We certainly didn't know if she could drive.

'My darlings, there's lots of things you don't know about me,' she said with a wink. 'Including, that I've always hankered after a camper-van.'

My brother said, 'But really, Sassy! Why pink?'

'If pink was good enough for Mr Singh and his family, then pink's good enough for us. Pink is the navy-blue of India.'

I said, 'So are we going camping?'

Sarsaparilla grinned. 'Who knows which way the wind bloweth?' She tried to look mysterious. This only made her look shifty. At once, we could tell there was a definite plan on the boil.

By Wednesday, Sarsaparilla had taken Mr Singh his thirty quid and got Ralph (who was my brother's dad) to get the van towed to a friend's lock-up garage to be rehabilitated.

'The trouble with her is her heart's always been bigger than her wallet,' said Ralph with a shrug.

Not just her heart. Everything about her was bigger than average. Sense of fun. Thirst for adventure. Creative impulses. And sheer physical bulk.

Like a ten-ton truck, she came revving towards whatever she was about to covet and collect, and you had to duck for fear that your rib-cage would crack under pressure from those massive, wobbling, out-stretched arms wanting to hug you back to life.

Because, you must understand, she also collected rattletrap people. And I was one of them.

She had so much affection to give. Being loved by Sarsaparilla made you safe and enfolded. And I tried to love her back, of course I did. But being loved by someone doesn't necessarily mean you like living with them all the time and putting up with their ever-changing life-plans.

Always, there was some new scheme hidden up her copious sleeve. It could be utterly exhausting. And these schemes could lead to distressing things happening as well as benign. As I will, in due course, reveal.

Our Cosy Family Circle

My brother Daniel was Sarsaparilla's natural and born-to-her son. The rest of us were her collectables. If you're a collectable yourself, you'll know what it's like, even if you use a different term in your own household.

And if you don't know, because you happen to be living with your blood mother or blood father, or your gran, or your foster auntie, or in a boarding school or some other institution of containment and correction, then this account of some turbulent times from family life will elucidate how being a collectable can sometimes offer the worst aspects of childhood, yet at other times can provide the most liberating childhood experience of all.

I'd lived with Sassy as my sort-of parent for so long that most people at school thought she must be my real mother.

'Listen you!' I'd say. 'She's not even the right to call herself my *step*mother!'

She and my blood father were never married to each

other. They'd cohabited as a loving couple for a brief time when my father was on his own with me. I expect Sarsaparilla felt sorry for him. When he moved on, he left me behind in a legally ambiguous situation. He believed he was doing the right thing by me. Apparently, he thought it'd be better for his little girl to have the stability of normal family life. How could he have believed that life with Sarsaparilla would be stable or normal?

I don't remember the break-up. I might have cried. But probably I didn't for, not only is it in my nature to try to be cheerful in all situations, but also because Sarsaparilla would certainly have gathered me up and squeezed me to her squishy front and murmured into my ear how she would love me always and for ever and ever amen, until the end of time and then some more, just as she'd done to my sisters, Elizabeth, Georgie, Edwina, and Tilly, and I would have been comforted.

We five girls were all collectables. This, as Georgie pointed out, made Sarsaparilla *more* our mother, not less.

'You see, *we've* each been personally chosen. Poor sad Daniel merely occurred as an unstoppable fact of nature, didn't you, Dannyboy? You actually had to slide, all slimy, from her body.'

'Ssswhasssat? Ssswhadyamean?' Edwina, jumping up and down like a mad flea, asked. She spoke with an absurd and confusing superfluity of esses because she was missing three of her top teeth. Two came out in the normal way for people of her age. One had been most unfortunately knocked out during a family game on the stairs which I knew, even at the time, was going to end in blood and physical damage to somebody and I was just hoping it wouldn't be me.

Seven is supposed to be the age of reason. But Edwina was seldom reasonable. She was always getting in people's way and she was always asking her silly questions.

'Ssswhadyaonabout now? I don't get it,' she persisted. Then, when Georgie explained she was talking about Daniel's birth, she said, 'Ssseergh! Sssatss's disssgusssting!'

By her age, Edwina should have already known the bald facts of the reproductive processes. We'd told her enough times. But she was distressed by Georgie's enthusiasm for detailed description. Georgie enjoyed recounting gory births, and specially Daniel's, which was the only one we knew about. (Sarsaparilla had told us, and him, how he arrived in the middle of the night, on a cold stone kitchen floor, by the light of an open wood fire, with no doctor or nurse present, only the local dairy farmer's wife to act as midwife.)

Georgie relished reminding Daniel of this event. She liked the way it made Daniel blink, then blush, then look away as though he wished the angels on high would gather him up. He was an immature person. Boys mature later than girls. However, he had all those hormones swishing hopefully about his body endeavouring to change him into a youth, if not into a man.

'Weird, isn't it?' Georgie persisted. She was ten and her hormones hadn't yet started doing any noticeable swishing. 'To think of being *born* out of someone you know!'

I said, 'Though being born out of someone you *don't* know is even weirder.' Neither Georgie nor I were in touch with our natural mothers. Mine had died. Georgie's had failed to care for her in the way that the state believed a mother should and the court had stuck an Interim Care Order on her.

Georgie said thoughtfully, 'Thinking about the time *before* you were born, maybe that's the weirdest of all? Just swimming about in murky fluid, looking like a sea-horse, feeling bored, with no one to talk to.'

Daniel listened to, but did not join in with these informative female chats. He was a timid, gentle human. Sometimes I wished I'd shown him more affection when I still had the chance.

How Mrs Jeans Made Bubbles

On Wednesday afternoon, at the same moment that Sarsaparilla was handing over her wad of fivers to Mr Singh, I was ordered out of the classroom. Miss Phillp told me to go to the Special Inclusion Unit until I'd calmed down and learned to behave. I wasn't surprised. It was always happening to me, though as far as I could see, it had nothing to do with having Sarsaparilla as my parent.

'Directly,' said Miss Phillp sharply. 'No dilly-dallying.'

The Special Inclusion Unit was where pupils got sent if they were considered to be difficult, disruptive, or disaffected. It was a stuffy room with frosted glass windows so you couldn't see out. Nobody could see in either. This was supposed to offer the disgraced person privacy but everybody knew who they were from the way they'd been behaving in class.

Being sent to the SIU was like entering a lottery. As chancy as life itself. Sometimes you got a serious telling-off. Other times, you got to do jigsaws or look at books. It depended who was on duty and whether they considered doing 1,000-piece jigsaws with lots of the pieces missing was a punishment or a reward.

That day, since no one else in the entire school had been noticeably disruptive or disaffected, I was on my own. I didn't like that. I preferred being in the middle of a crowd. Alone, I wasn't a very interesting person. Moreover, as I was the sole pupil in the Special Inclusion Unit, I was obliged to sit and make conversation with the Visiting Welfare Officer.

I said, 'This isn't going to be much fun for you. We haven't got anything in common and I'm not a very entertaining person.'

The VWO said, 'It's my job.'

And it was. It transpired that she was paid to be nice to me, to find out why I was there, why I was the way I was, and if anything could be done about it.

She wouldn't let me sort out the muddled jigsaws. Or flick through the tatty books. Instead, she wanted me to draw.

'A map of your family.'

I said, 'A map? Are you sure, Mrs Jeans?' (I soon deduced that was her name because she wore a plastic identity badge pinned to her cardigan.)

She said, 'Yes, dear.' She knew me by sight even if she couldn't immediately recall my name. She can't have considered me to be dangerously disruptive or she'd have left the SIU door open so she could summon help. A few pupils weren't just disruptive. They could be destructive, too, and aggressive. Schools can be dangerous places for the meek. Sarsaparilla told me so. That's why she didn't approve of them, even though she made us go.

I said to Mrs Jeans, 'Families aren't usually mapped, are they?'

She said, 'It is sometimes called a "family tree". But I

12

find "map" is a more flexible term which better covers the vicissitudes of modern life.'

'Of course,' I said because I wasn't going to let her know that I hadn't a clue what vicissitudes were. 'I quite agree. Absolutely. Vicissitudes are essential.' I'd have to ask Daniel later to tell me about them.

'So I'll start you off.' She drew a bubble-shape on a clean sheet of paper. 'What's your name again, dear?' She was at a disadvantage. Pupils do not wear identifying badges.

'Jewells. Jewells Green. Actually, it's Julia. But everybody always calls me Jewells.'

She wrote 'Julia' in the middle of her sheet of paper. 'Now,' she said. 'You add the names of other significant relationships within your family unit and link them, within their own spheres, to one another, as appropriate.'

'Whassat?' I said, as though I was my kid sister with the missing teeth. Enclosing people in family bubbles was as far-fetched as sitting them like birds on the branches of family trees. 'Mrs Jeans, humans live in bubbles if they're seriously sick with immune deficiencies. Everyone at my home is entirely healthy.' Then I remembered how the mother-figure in my life had to take pills every day for her high blood pressure. I also remembered Mrs Churchill's scruffy little body lying on its back on the floor of the hamster cage, very dead.

I said, 'Except for Mrs Churchill who sadly passed away. But it was hardly a tragedy, except of course for Mr Churchill who is part of my family though no relation since he is a hamster. Hamsters are only supposed to live for a couple of years in human terms so Mrs Churchill's passing was hardly a surprise to anybody.'

Mrs Jeans said she was sorry if I found it painful. It was a voluntary exercise and she wouldn't force me. 'But it can be a most useful tool for self-discovery.'

Self-discovery sounded mildly interesting, like going on a journey. So I agreed to go along with her map. 'Specially if it makes you feel your day has been worthwhile, Mrs Jeans,' I added and smiled fetchingly with my head on one side like the Queen Mother did in those old news films. I wanted to show how co-operative I could be, for the longer I remained there, the less time I'd have to spend back in class with Miss Phillp and the Tudors.

'We done them before, way back with that supply teacher,' one of the boys had complained.

Tough. Miss Phillp wanted us to do them again. The Tudors were the only thing she knew about. The Tudors were OK by me. It was Miss Phillp's teaching manner that got me down.

You'd think that a rich, fat, over-sexed, sickly king called Henry who managed to have six wives would be an absorbing subject for a class of young people on the threshold of reproductive life. But Miss Phillp had a knack of making even Henry's personal relationships seem dreary.

I'd not intended to be disruptive. I'd merely been trying to liven things up for the benefit of the other pupils. But Miss Phillp had got in a strop and asked who was teaching this class, me or her?

Now, obligingly, I took a fresh sheet of Mrs Jeans's paper and drew a bubble with Sarsaparilla's name in the middle. Then, out near the edge, I drew a tiny me floating like a migratory bird on its voyage of self-discovery.

Mrs Jeans peered. 'Now, Julia,' she said. 'We're supposed to be talking about *you*. *You* should be at the centre of our relationship chart.'

I wasn't used to people talking about me. I should have explained to her that I preferred it when I was in a crowd with lots of people. On my own, I felt I was so uninteresting as to be almost invisible. But I didn't explain because I knew that a woman who wore brown tights, a fawn-coloured skirt, and had beige hair would never understand.

I said, 'Sarsaparilla's *always* in the middle. She is the glowing planet around which the rest of us must revolve.'

'Ah,' said Mrs Jeans, nodding hard. 'Ah yes.'

It wasn't me who'd first thought up such a poetical turn of phrase to describe a dominant mother but someone called Mick who fancied Sarsaparilla so much he used to leave orchids for her on her doorstep. I wrote Mick's name, then encircled it in its own bubble to demonstrate to Mrs Jeans that he was out of her life (and therefore mine) and had been for some time.

Half-heartedly, I added a few more names. But this system of over-lapping bubbles was making my family seem more confusing than it needed to be.

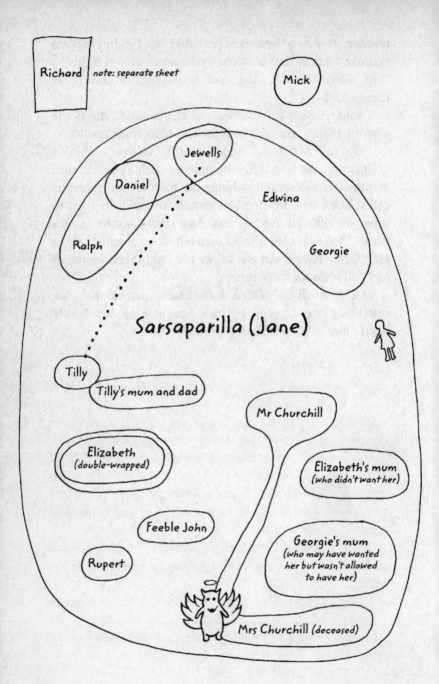

16

How I Made a Family Bubble

'Mrs Jeans,' I said, 'don't you think a list of names would be easier to follow? Like the class register?'

Even new teachers, straight out of college, managed to cope with the register. They knew how important it was.

'It can mean a matter of life and death,' a student teacher once told me.

I said, 'How come?' because I thought the register was to find out who was bunking off that day, which is rarely a matter of life or death.

The student said, 'It's in case of fire. The fire brigade must check how many people are still trapped inside the building.'

If there were to be a fire just then, Miss Phillp's register would claim I was in the classroom when in fact I'd be in the SIU with Mrs Jeans. Would the fire brigade find us in time?

I said, 'We'd have to get down on the floor and crawl along with hankies over our mouths to filter the smoke. The lower you are, the more air there is to breathe.'

Mrs Jeans looked at me curiously. She didn't understand that I was telling her how we might escape in the event of fire.

I resolved not to confuse her further. The bubbles within bubbles were already muddling enough for both of us. The more I added the more she nodded.

In normal circumstances, a nod of the head exchanged between two humans, and sometimes even between a human and an intelligent animal such as a dog, or a horse, or a donkey, though not between two hamsters because, however intelligent they may think they are, their necks are too short for nodding, signifies Affirmative. However, I observed that a Mrs-Jeans-nod indicated the reverse. It meant, 'No, I do not understand a word of what is being said by this person.'

Now she began to shake her head vigorously from side to side. 'So if I understand what you're saying, you are the third child of six?'

'Uhuh. Correct,' I said because if I'd nodded she might have interpreted it as a No.

'That must be a lot of work for your mother?'

'No. Sarsaparilla doesn't look after us. She can't. She's a painter.' Not that I'd noticed her anywhere near a painting for months. 'I mean, she's more of a situation artist. An artist of the quotidian. Besides, we don't need looking after. We look after ourselves. We practise Domestic Democracy.'

Mrs Jeans nodded, indicating negative comprehension.

'You know,' I elaborated. 'An I for an I. Independence for Infants. Freedom to make our own mistakes.' I thought all parents knew about stuff like that. But it seems II was an invention of Sarsaparilla's.

'And your father? Where is he on the map?'

'Father!' I spluttered.

She tried again with a variant of father in case I hadn't understood. 'Daddy?' she said tentatively.

I made another splutter. Only molly-coddled girls with ponies and pink sparkle trainers use the daddy-word, or so Sarsaparilla said.

'Of course I had a father,' I said coldly. 'I wasn't created in a Petri-dish. But I don't keep up with him any more.' The truth was, *he* didn't keep up with *me*. He'd dumped me in the chaos of Sarsaparilla's rattletrap household and, though there were birthday cards and presents from time to time, he never came to see me.

Mrs Jeans looked so disappointed, neither nodding nor shaking, that I relented. 'All right, if you insist. His name's Richard.' I wrote 'Richard' for her on a separate sheet of paper. I carried it across the room and placed it on a chair by the door. 'See. He's out of it. Faraway. He's a business person. He runs factories that make extruders.'

'Very well, dear. Next step then, I'd like you to talk me through these special people of yours. Tell me about each of them. What do they mean to you?'

'What d'you *mean*, what do they mean? People don't mean anything. They just are.' I snatched the sheet from her. 'Oh, very well then, if I must. I'll start in the middle. Once upon a time there was an art student; in those days, she was called Jane.' I jabbed my finger on Sarsaparilla's name. I wrote 'Jane' under it. 'She met Ralph. They fell in love. They had a boy baby, my brother, Daniel Green.'

In my family, as it then was, we all called ourselves The Greens even though most of us hadn't a drop of Green blood in our veins.

'Daniel's in Year 9. D'you know what his name means?'

Mrs Jeans nodded her irritating negative.

19

'Judged of God. That's quite a heavy responsibility, isn't it? Though my nan told me that everybody will be judged at the last trump.'

I didn't think Mrs Jeans was listening. She was too busy scribbling away in her notebook as single-mindedly as Mr Churchill on his exercise wheel.

I knew she wouldn't know Daniel from Adam. He was quietly studious, rarely disruptive, and never got sent to the SIU. 'He should be in Year 8. But he's terribly brainy. He doesn't have any friends. Lazy boys hate brainy boys.'

One of the amazing things about Daniel was that he went on getting good marks for his work even though we didn't have a computer, nor a video-player, let alone DVD, mobiles, a camcorder, or any of that useful stuff. Sarsaparilla insisted it was up to us to discover the complex wonders of the universe without the intrusion of technology. We didn't even have a television, not since it caught fire in a thunderstorm. An act of God, the insurers called it. An act of mercy and deliverance according to Sarsaparilla.

I said, 'We used to have another brother. Rupert. He was ever so sweet. He must be nearly five by now. But one day, a woman came in a taxi, put all his things in a black bin bag and took him away.'

'Maybe she was his social worker?' said Mrs Jeans. 'Perhaps it was only meant to be an interim placement.'

I knew Mrs Jeans didn't understand. A lot of people didn't. They thought that rattletrap families didn't have feelings like the rest of the population. They thought you got used to arrivals and departures. But you never did.

'She was a *kidnapper*. She kidnapped him,' I said, 'and we haven't seen him since. How would you feel if it happened to you?'

Happy Ever After

'So then,' I said, 'they married.'

'You've lost me there, dear. Who did?'

I knew she'd have found a list simpler to follow. 'Ralph and Sarsaparilla, of course. She wanted loads more children. She's a baby-aholic. However, Ralph already had Elizabeth left over from his first marriage. She's his stepdaughter. His first wife found her difficult to love because of her being so intellectually challenged.' I dabbed my finger firmly on Elizabeth's name. 'We don't know what she's thinking most of the time because having a brain like hers is like wearing two pairs of rubber gloves.'

Mrs Jeans raised her eyebrows. 'VIRUS PHOBIA????' she wrote in big letters on her pad. 'Why might one choose to wear *two* pairs, dear?'

This woman really was very slow. 'When you're washing-up, of course. Because Sarsaparilla won't buy us a dishwasher. She says they're ecologically unsound. We have a rota instead. It's always my turn. Daniel fiddles it,

I'm sure he does. When you know there's a hole in one of the gloves but you can't find it, you either have to fill them with water and see where it drips out, or you wear two pairs. It makes your hands feel foggy, and that's what Elizabeth's mind is like.'

The bell went. Mrs Jeans looked incredibly relieved. She stood up. She picked up the bubble chart as though it was a rare navigational aid and slid it inside a folder.

'Hey, but wait, I haven't finished telling you.' I spoke fast to get it all in. 'Elizabeth's-been-with-Sarsaparilla-even-longer-than-Daniel,- she-came-with-Ralph-and-when-he-changed-his-mind-about-Jane-which-was-something-to-do-with-her-changing-her-name-to-Sarsaparilla-and-went-off-with-Lulu, everybody, even-the-social-worker, decided-Elizabeth-better-stay-where-she-was-because-she'd-got-settled, and-Lulu-certainly-didn't-want-Elizabeth-and-Daniel-messing-up-her-life, though-when-she-found-out-she-couldn't-have-babies-of-her-own, she changed-her-mind-about-Daniel, but-it-was-too-late-because-he-didn't-want-to-go-and-live-with-his-stepmother-even-if-it-meant-he-could-be-with-his-father.'

Along the corridor beyond the frosted glass came the powerful surge of humanity as classes emptied and the contents flooded towards the cloakrooms.

'Thank you, dear,' said Mrs Jeans. 'You've already shed a great deal of light on your situation. I'm beginning to understand where you're coming from and what makes you tick.'

I was affronted at being cut short. 'The larger the family, the longer the telling of their story must take,' I said. 'Also, I am not a clock. So I do not tick.'

But I was. And I did.

'Very well then, dear,' said Mrs Jeans, pausing in the doorway. 'Tell me one more thing, what are your feelings for your foster mother? Would you say you loved her?'

I shouldn't have answered. But she sprang it on me. Without reflecting, I said, 'Sassy? Oh no. She's a terrible parent. I wouldn't wish her on my worst enemy,' and the words quivered in the air like shards of broken glass. The trouble with saying something cruel is that you start to believe it's true.

I swam against the human flow back to my classroom. I collected my bag. I bumped into Miss Phillp.

'Aha, Julia. Better now?' she asked. I felt ticking inside me like a primed explosive device.

Tick-tock. Disruption, disaffection.

Tick-tock. Discord, disobedience.

Tickety-tock. Disorder, dysfunction.

All were waiting to erupt. The hormones of puberty were swishing about inside my body causing chaos. I felt the pressure of the walls. I sniffed the staleness of the air. I saw the grey moustache on Miss Phillp's upper lip. Her hormones were swishing too.

'Well, good afternoon, Julia. See you tomorrow.'

I said nothing. I'm not a deliberately rude person. If I'd known I wouldn't be seeing her again, I might've been more civil.

I stomped down to the Girls' cloakrooms. How would I survive another six years in this claustrophobic institution?

Outside, at the school gate, I came upon Daniel. He was lurking in the shadows because he'd been crying. He was still snivelling, in a feeble, weasel-like way.

'I suppose you think *you've* had an even worse day than me?' I snarled.

He had. A larger boy had scribbled on his perfect homework. Someone else had stamped on the fountain pen which Ralph had given him for his birthday till it cracked and bled ink all over his hands. The Greens may have been peculiar but we didn't go in for inter-personal violence.

'Oh, grow up, Daniel! Be a man! It's not that bad!' I said. Even though he's eleven months older than me, he sometimes needed encouragement.

He only cried more. So I gave him the briefest of hugs. I said I'd loan him one of my Bics.

'Thanks,' he sniffed. Even when his fountain pen hadn't been jumped on, he was like a bag of sad stones. I liked him anyway.

We shuffled home side-by-side through the gloaming in sibling silence. Neither of us knew how, even at that moment, Sarsaparilla was bringing one of her creative life-plans into action so that Daniel and I would never have to go to school again.

Furtive Get-away

The changes began next morning at 07.13 according to the glowing red digital numbers on the clock on the front of the electric cooker. Sarsaparilla came bustling into the kitchen in one of those gaudy floral smocks she liked to make herself out of curtains from the charity shop.

That was the first shock. Not the eye-catching brilliance of her outfit but the fact that she was conscious and up and about so early. Usually, when we left for school, she was still asleep. Granting us our I for I, Independence for Infants, as she liked to call it, though we all knew perfectly well it was because she enjoyed a lie-in under the covers as much as the next person.

She gave me a good morning hug, crushing my cheeks into the folds of the yellow chrysanthemums on her dress.

I gasped for air. She released me. 'You gorgeous girl. And how are you coming along then?'

She didn't mean How-Are-you-Coming-Along-with-your-Schoolwork-and-Progressing-in-the-Maturing-Processes, so I didn't tell her about my session in the SIU the day before. That could wait till next parents' evening when, whatever derogatory things the teachers might say about me, I could rely on Sarsaparilla to defend me to the last moment, then I'd tell her afterwards how I'd misbehaved.

Sarsaparilla peered down at the four mighty mounds of roughly sliced bread lying like sections of Hadrian's Wall on the kitchen surface. She meant, How are you coming along with the packed lunches?

It was another of Daniel's rota fiddles that I was on Green's Nutrition Duty all week. It was my task to prepare seventeen cheese and raw spinach leaf sandwiches. Four for Daniel, five for Georgie, six for Edwina, to build her up because she was so weedy and pale. Her skin was almost translucent. You could see her veins with the blood trickling along like blue paint-water. Only two sandwiches for me. I was verging on the chunky and thought if I pretended to eat less, it might make a difference. I refused to accept that it was about the swishing hormones and the not joining in with sports. I was yet to learn that ceaseless physical exercise, such as digging water-logged earth and chopping wet firewood, enables the human body to consume billions of calories yet remain streamlined.

'Six, seven, eight. Fine,' I said, sandwich-counting. 'Nine, ten, eleven. Nearly there.'

Sarsaparilla discouraged us from testing out the canteen meals which, she claimed, were filled with E-coli, monosodium glutamate, BSEs, salmonella, atramazines, foot-and-mouth diseases, brucelosis, blight, botulism, chicken-pox. She may have been right.

I wrapped the sandwiches in their appropriate packs. I added a peeled raw carrot to each. Most days, I managed to swap my own healthy, beta carotene-packed carrot stick with one of the class anorexics for a packet of M&Ms so that she'd get her vitamin A and I'd get my instant sugar burst. If Sarsaparilla found out, I'd explain that I was exercising my right to I for I.

'Hurry up, Jewells, angel, because we're all set.'

'Set?' I said. 'How d'you mean? It's not Saturday.' On Saturdays, just when I fancied a lie-in, she usually had some surprise excursion to the recycling centre or to a community street clear-up or to help out on the stalls at a church jumble sale.

'To start our new life, cherub,' said Sarsaparilla, as though I ought to have known, and she scuttled off to pack bundles of clean wet washing into a bin-bag.

'We're moving,' said Georgie, passing behind me and nicking one of the sandwiches that was poking through its wrapping. 'Didn't you know?'

'No. Why should I? Nobody ever tells me anything. Where to?'

The trouble with living with a person who kept surprises up her sleeve and schemes on the boil is that they always thought they'd told you more than they had. So you were left groping in the dark for a fuller understanding.

'Dunno. Think Daniel knows. Something to do with mind-body-spirit. Whatever that might be. She wants to miss rush-hour.'

Georgie co-operated with Sarsaparilla's schemes because if she protested, the Local Authority might move her to another foster mother who might turn out to be mean, cruel, and generally wicked. Whatever people said about Sarsaparilla behind her back, they never said she was any of those.

Daniel was outside loading things onto the roof-rack. Edwina stood around sucking the wispy ends of her orange hair and getting in people's way. Georgie scurried to help Tilly and Elizabeth get their shoes on.

I said, 'If we're moving, what's the point of me making all these sandwiches?'

Georgie said, 'You're supposed to be bringing them. We'll need sustenance on the trip.'

'A tricksss!' said Edwina. 'I do like tricksss. Whasss sssort of triksss?'

'Trick trick hooray!' said Tilly, clapping her hands with anticipation.

Thanks to some new light-bulbs, reconditioned brake-linings, and salvaged windscreen wipers, the pink camper-van had passed its road safety test. When Sarsaparilla started up the engine, it threw out black smoke, then moved forward. We were all astonished at her skill as a driver. We chugged through the suburban rush-hour and got as far as the second set of traffic lights when Georgie whispered, 'What about Feeble John?'

I whispered back, 'I think he'll be glad when he finds we've gone away and he can get on with the rest of his feeble life in peace.'

Feeble John was Sarsaparilla's ex-person-friend. None of us liked him. Not even Sarsaparilla any more. He wasn't anybody's father or stepfather. He liked Sarsaparilla a lot. But he didn't understand kids.

Georgie whispered, 'He'll be ever so sad.'

I whispered, 'Not in the long run. It was bound to fail.'

We went out of town and across the industrial estate. As we passed Toys'R'Us, Comet, and B & Q, stuffed with the consumer durables that we weren't supposed to yearn for, Sarsaparilla made us shout and boo. Back in class, right then, they'd just be starting the register. I was glad I wasn't there. I was glad I was here, secure inside this pink, rusting, van-shaped bubble. Here were precisely the right number of names, safe and cosy against the outside world.

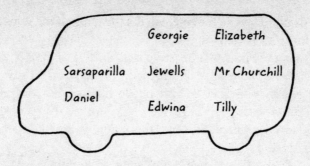

Georgie   Elizabeth

Sarsaparilla   Jewells   Mr Churchill

Daniel   Edwina   Tilly

In our own unique way, we Greens formed the ideal family. We didn't need anybody else around. If only our perfect bubble could have lasted forever.

When We Were
on the Road

The journey was long. We munched our way through the carrot sticks. We shared out the cheese and spinach sandwiches. Elizabeth was sick. We played I-spy. Tilly had a snooze. Edwina and Georgie had a scuffle. Daniel led us in singing sixty verses of 'The Animals Went into the Ark' until we ran out of the names of beasts of the fields, birds of the air, fowls of the farmyard, fishes of the seas, and insects of the undergrowth. I wondered how soon before Sarsaparilla would turn back. Frequently, her escapades terminated almost before they'd begun.

Daniel was supposed to be map-reading. But Sarsaparilla kept contradicting his instructions.

'Turn *left*, did I hear you say?' she said. 'No, dear heart, that cannot possibly be correct. It's a straight-on. I can feel how the van wants to go straight ahead. It knows the way. By instinct. It's obviously been down here before, in a previous life.'

'Of course it hasn't. For fifteen years, it's been backwards and forwards to Leicester visiting Mr Singh's relatives.'

Sarsaparilla said, 'I daresay, sweetheart, you're reading your map upside-down.'

'No I'm not,' said Daniel. 'We did all this last term.'

'Did what? Came *here*?' said Sarsaparilla, disbelievingly.

We had to accept all her stuff about old vans having long memories, yet she rarely believed straightforward stuff we told her about perfectly ordinary lessons that happened at school.

'Of course not. I mean, we learned about map-reading and orienteering. It's part of geography.'

Sarsaparilla was as surprised as if he'd said he'd taken up tap-dancing. 'How perfectly extraordinary. I had no idea they taught you anything of practical use.'

Daniel was more tolerant of her constant niggling than ever he was with louts who teased him or jumped on his pens. Perhaps because she was his mother. Perhaps because he loved her in some invisible male way that we didn't know about.

A tractor pulled out in front of us. Sarsaparilla's driving was as erratic as her schemes. She swung past, blaring the horn. Nothing must inhibit the impetus of her chosen trajectory until she herself was ready to stop. (That wasn't my expression. It was Ralph who first said it. Even though he wasn't my father, or even anything to do with me, I liked some of his turns of phrase. If I'd *had* to have a father living nearby, I'd have chosen Ralph.)

Mr Churchill began scrabbling nervously through the chewed-up newspaper in the bottom of his cage.

'I think he's feeling travel sick,' said Georgie.

Tilly woke and started grizzling. I wiped my thumb and gave it to her to suck. I was impressed how interested a tiny tot could be in playing with a thumb, even when it was another person's.

When Sarsaparilla's cosmic energy ran out, she had to admit that we were lost. I dared ask if she had even the faintest clue where she was taking us.

'Oh, you child of little faith, of course I do! We're escaping the relentless treadmill of modern urbanity in order to seek the Eden of intellectual freedom and the paradise of rural purity.'

'Ssshassat?' Edwina hissed through her toothless top gum. 'Whasssatt Sssassy'sss on about?'

'You'll see when we get there, sweetie-pie. And you'll be thrilled beyond measure.'

I didn't hold with children as young as Edwina being kept waiting for essential factual information concerning their future lives so I told Edwina, 'Paradise and Eden are both grown-up words for heaven. So we're going to some type of heaven place.'

'Sssat mean we gonna die today?' Edwina asked. The discovery of Mrs Churchill's lifeless body in the cage had been just one week earlier. Edwina was still preoccupied with the topic.

'Of course not! Only hamsters die unexpectedly, and even they only do that when they're exceedingly old.' I gave her a reassuring hug to distract her from the fact that I was lying on two counts.

One. Mrs Churchill had not been old, even in hamster terms.

Two. Nor had my first mother, yet she had died most unexpectedly, twelve hours after I was born. On my birthday I'd made the mistake of confiding in a girl at school the sad circumstances of my blood mother's demise shortly after my own arrival in the world, in the hope of eliciting sympathy. 'Must've been the shock of setting eyes on a weirdo like you!' the girl said laughing like a parrot before swaggering off to make friends with some other girls who were more sophisticated than I.

Sarsaparilla was right. School was a vile place to waste the worst days of one's youth. I was well out of it.

We Who Would Valiant Be

Sarsaparilla pulled off the road by a lonely farm in a bleak and threatening landscape.

'Lovely sunset, isn't it? Now stay tight, my little chitterlings. I'll just pop in here and ask for directions.'

I didn't see any sunset. But twilight was definitely gathering round us like a shroud. We could hear Mr Churchill, for whom dusk was dawn, get up and begin running around his cage and playing on his little plastic circus toys. Despite his grief, he always kept himself active and cheerful. Daniel took out his maths books and worked on his homework by torchlight. He said he was doing algebra. I didn't even know what that was.

'*Don't* you?' he said with surprise as though I'd said I didn't know what pencils were.

I said, 'Looks more like you're learning how to write Egyptian.'

'Algebra's a method of working things out by equation. The foundations were laid down in eight hundred and twenty-five by an Islamic mathematician, Muhammad Ibn Musa al-Khwarizmi.'

'I don't geddit,' said Edwina.

'Nor do I,' I said.

'I'll explain it to you if you like?'

It was so annoying, the way he knew so much more than I ever would. He didn't mean to show off but he couldn't ever keep his superior knowledge to himself.

'No thanks,' I said coldly. 'I have no idea why you're bothering to finish your homework when you won't be there to hand it in.'

He grinned. 'Because it's fun.'

Sarsaparilla came billowing out of the murk like a large floral ghost.

'Nearly there! Nearly there!' she trilled, climbing back into the driver's seat. 'Oh, it's so terribly exciting. You're all going to adore it. Absolutely. Did I tell you, darlings, it has its own meadow, and orchard, and a barn so we can keep a cow.'

'A cow?'

'Or a goat. Goat milk's said to be wonderful for soothing eczema.'

None of us had eczema. The only spotty skin around was the acne on Daniel's forehead which he tried to keep hidden behind a heavy forelock of slightly greasy brown hair.

'And you'll never guess what,' Sarsaparilla went on enthusiastically. 'There's a copper in the old laundry so whoever's on laundry duty can boil up our clothes in wood-ash.'

'Ssswhysss that?' asked Edwina.

'Because, my petal, that's what they used to do in the olden days.'

'So why will we have to do it?' I asked.

'Because you wouldn't want to go on destroying the

rivers and waterways with nasty chemical detergents, would you? And you'll find there's a yard at the back where you can hang the washing to dry in the sun. And we'll keep hens and ducks, shan't we, and there's a walled garden where we'll grow radishes and lettuces and strawberries and—'

Elizabeth recognized her favourite word. 'Stawb!' she crowed. 'Like 'em I do.'

'Stawbee!' echoed Tilly who also knew the word, and she clapped her hands and gurgled, as merry as a little drain in a big monsoon.

'That's right, buttercup. You shall feast on freshly gathered strawberries every morning, glistening red and ripe upon your porridge.' Sarsaparilla sounded so excited and lovely and warm and motherly that I yearned for everything she told us to be true.

'All hail and glory to the strawberry,' I sang and the others soon joined in with the chorus of one of our sillier Green songs, all except for Daniel who said in a low voice, 'The successful soft fruit bed requires a large quantity of well-rotted manure and until we acquire that cow we won't have the necessary soil nutrients to hand.'

But sitting in the dark in the back of the van it was easy enough to ignore him. None of us gave a thought to the fact that the only strawberries likely to be fruiting in February would be in Dutch glasshouses across the North Sea.

The camper-van lurched us down a track, bumpy and overgrown. In the beam of headlights we saw a signboard dangling lop-sidedly off a nail on a tree.

BEWAR O
THE G

Whatever there was to beware of couldn't be confirmed because the bottom half of the board had gone.

'Been nibbled by bunnies,' said Georgie who knew even less of country life than I did.

'Don't be daft!' I said. 'Rabbits are vegetarian.'

'Wood isn't meat.'

'All right. But rabbits don't eat wood. Nothing eats wood.' I had no reason to be aggressive. Yet sometimes I couldn't help provoking her into an argument.

'Yes they do,' said Georgie. 'Some animals love eating wood.'

'Name one,' I said.

'Ants.'

'All right. Ants. But that's all.'

'And beavers.'

'You don't get beavers here. You're thinking of badgers who eat worms but never wood.'

Georgie had taken up the challenge of my provocation. 'And chipmunks definitely.'

'Nor chipmunks.'

'And what about woodlice then? That's why they're called that.'

I said, 'You don't have to eat what you're called. Butterflies don't eat butter. Swordfish don't eat swords. Chipmunks don't eat chips.'

'Chisps!' crowed Elizabeth, hearing her second favourite word after strawberries. 'Like 'em I do.'

'Jewells is right, girls,' said Daniel, unexpectedly taking my side. Here's a curious and wondrous fact about sibling rivalry. Just when you think you've sussed out which person is your chief adversary, that's the one who turns out to be your current ally. 'It's a common misapprehension that beavers consume wood. In fact, they gnaw trees in order to fell them so that they may build dams, within which they make their nests, which are known as lodges and which is where they raise their young.'

Georgie was now the ignorant loser. But I didn't like to see her so easily defeated so I felt for her hand in the dark and gave it a squeeze. She snatched it away.

'Don't touch me like that, Jewells. It's disgusting,' she hissed. 'People will think we're lesboes.'

What people? I thought. I said, 'OK. I won't ever touch you again. Not even to untangle your hair if you beg me. But I just wanted you to know that we all know Daniel knows too much. But it's not really his fault. He got given the wrong name when he was born. He should've been called Ernest.'

Georgie gave me a friendly biff in the ribcage.

Edwina said, 'Ernesst? I don't get it.'

In the front, Daniel shouted a warning to his mother. 'Watch out! Fallen log!' Too late. She drove into it anyway and the camper-van came to a juddering halt.

We'd arrived.

'Everybody out, my precious chickadees,' said Sarsaparilla in a voice which I could tell was smiling tenderly through the rural darkness. 'Elysian Fields, where we shall dwell henceforth in freedom and tranquillity.' She slid open the driver's door, letting in a whoosh of damp air which circulated round our legs. 'Where we may create our own ashram for the development of mind-body-spirit.'

'Ashram?'

'Retreat for spiritual growth.'

None of us had experience of spiritual growth, nor of retreating. Nor had we known, till then, that come the night, the real countryside is quite so black. No street-lamps, no shop-fronts, no flicking advertising screens. Not even the comforting orange glow of a distant motorway.

So we sat tight in the van, nobody budging. Something in the great outdoors squarked. We all jumped and huddled closer.

'Come along, my sweetings,' Sarsaparilla's voice coaxed out of the clammy night.

'Too dark,' said Georgie in a tiny croak.

'Then you must learn to make friends with darkness, my honeybun. Live in harmony with her.'

Tilly was first to venture to the open door. She sniffed at the cold air with her pink button nose, then rolled courageously out into the nothingness like a parachutist falling from a plane.

Sarsaparilla picked her up and set her back on her little feet.

So we followed, landed like a nest of writhing snakes in a tangle of brambles, struggled out of them, and made it to the door of our new home. Inside, there was no heating, precious little furniture, one bare electric light hanging from the ceiling, and an unpleasant smell.

Only Mr Churchill seemed unperturbed by the unfamiliar precariousness of our new life situation. He went on rummaging round the floor of his cage for lost husks and crusty flakes. I envied him, a hamster with no sibling responsibilities. He didn't even have to clean out his own cage.

On our first night of the mind-body-spirit experience, we had baked beans for supper which we ate cold, straight out of the tins.

The light flickered off, on, and off again, before quivering halfway between on and off. Sarsaparilla lit a candle and stuck it in a bottle. 'Isn't this too deliciously romantic?' she crooned.

Nobody dared reply.

The Itty Kitties

Sarsaparilla dissolved into the smelly shadows. We heard her plodding down a creaking corridor, humming.

'Isss ssso dark here,' whimpered a frail sibilant voice right beside me, and a clammy hand reached for mine.

The light flickered on again.

'For goodness' sake, Edwina!' I snapped. 'You're not the *only* person inhabiting this world. Try not to be so egocentric about everything.' One has to impart a few particles of etiquette to younger sisters if they're not to grow up totally selfish, though perhaps I was a bit harsh, for Edwina began to sob. 'What I meant was,' I said more gently, 'that everybody's always a bit uncertain about what lies ahead of them in life. And it's not that dark, either.'

The electric bulb flickered. Edwina started to snivel. It's disgusting to hear someone snivel in the dark because you know that as soon as the light comes on again, you'll find them all snotty and smeary up against your jumper.

However, I was saved from having Edwina's nose

products being rubbed on to my clothes by Daniel who wasn't just an academic brainhead. He was inventive too. He could think up strange distracting games in a nano-sec.

'I've an idea. Let's become pot-holers!' he said, switching off the light so it had to stay off. 'They're always in the dark. They like it that way. Get down on the floor everybody. We'll explore this deep subterranean tunnel which I sense is ahead.'

I found him, by feeling. He was already face-down on the cold stone floor waving his arms about as though feeling for the sides of the cave. So we joined him down there and squirmed along behind him, head to feet like a trail of processionary caterpillars.

Our eyes grew accustomed to the dark. We reached a storeroom. That's where the bad smell was coming from. The enclosed space was frisky with cats, a large old tabby and six skittish kittens. Their home was in amongst the flour bins, scurrying beetles, and squiggling centipedes.

'Iss loadsssa itty kittiessss!' said Edwina, her fear dissipated. 'I'sss having one for myssself.' She made a grab for the nearest.

She wasn't the only one who yearned for some small fluffy creature of her own to lavish tenderness upon. Unfortunately, the kittens weren't so keen to be cherished as we were to cherish them. They scratched and fought and their tiny claws, sharp as scimitars, jagged our skin like brambles.

'Change of game?' suggested Daniel and we became game-hunters stalking our quarry through impenetrable jungle.

Georgie managed to catch all the kittens and handed them out like Christmas gifts so we each had one, except Tilly who tried to hold hers by its tail so it escaped.

The tabby turned her back on the systematic kidnapping of her children. She padded wearily away to sit alone inside a roll of wire netting. The kitten which had escaped from Tilly's grasp tried to follow the mother cat. But she turned on it angrily and lashed out with a paw. The rebuffed kitten mewed pathetically.

I wondered, might Sarsaparilla ever be tempted to disown me like that? And if she did, what would I do? Sarsaparilla spoke often of the bedrock of love, and the sustaining power of EMA (enduring maternal attachment). But if your primary mother has abandoned you, for whatever reason, even when it wasn't deliberate, you can't help mulling things over.

I tried not to mull too often. Sarsaparilla's mum had warned me against it. But it made me so sad to observe this cat's unmaternal behaviour (and I'm not normally a very observant person, as Miss Phillp used to tell me). It reminded me of the behaviour of Elizabeth's blood mother. And Edwina's. Two mothers who wilfully rejected their daughters.

I was glad my mother hadn't done that. Straightforward puerperal dying was without blame or blemish. Or so Sarsaparilla's mum told me.

I'd intended not to mull but sometimes, once you start thinking, you can't stop yourself. I knew it was a sign of weakness to let your emotions out, especially in front of your foster siblings.

I heard Sarsaparilla calling, searching for us. 'Yoo-hoo, my cherubs! Where are you?' At once, my secret sadness melted. Everything was all right. We Greens, safe inside our perfect bubble, were, in our own unique way, the perfect family.

Or so I thought.

Sarsaparilla

Georgie + 1 kitty   Elizabeth + 1 kitty
Daniel + 1 kitty   Jewells + 1 kitty

        Tilly   Edwina + 1 kitten
             Mr Churchill

How We Coped with Fear and Dirt

Later that night when I was cowering in a strange room, on a strange lumpy mattress on an unfamiliar iron bedstead, I heard a whisper asking for me.

'Jewells? Jewells? You awake?'

'Yes.'

It was Georgie. 'I just remembered something.'

'What?'

'It's ever so bad. I don't know if I should tell you.'

'You might as well, now you've started.' I was expecting a confession of some sin so small it was almost invisible, like nicking another person's pencil-sharpener.

''S about Elizabeth.'

'What's she done?'

'Not her. It's what other people did. Used to do, in the olden days. It was seeing that cat reminded me. They took people like Elizabeth outside the city walls and *left* them

43

there, on the bare mountainside, to be consumed by wolves. Isn't that just *awful?*'

I agreed that it was and we spent a few solemn moments thinking about it together till Georgie said, 'She wouldn't have been angry though, would she?'

I'd just begun to fall asleep at last. 'Wouldn't what?'

'Elizabeth. When they took her up to the bare rock?'

'No. Don't suppose so.' Elizabeth was never angry, though she had plenty of reason to be, being born with a strange brain, and being dumped by her blood mother.

'She'd have gone on sitting there, smiling, as the wolves came towards her, wouldn't she?'

Imagining our dear trusting Elizabeth grinning mystically towards an approaching pack of wolves on a lonely mountainside was far worse than being brought to a dark damp house called Heaven and being expected to like it. The image we'd conjured up made Georgie and me both start to cry even though Elizabeth was in fact alive and well and snoring in bed right between us.

In the modern world, there were still people who believed that girls like Elizabeth who would never—short of a miracle in which I don't happen to believe—be able to take care of themselves, oughtn't to be allowed to use up valuable time and resources in the world.

They didn't put them on rocks but they disposed of them before they were born. Georgie and I both knew about it. Sarsaparilla's mum had told us and the disposal of unwanted babies had become part of Georgie's select repertoire of gory gynaecological tales. We didn't say anything more about it in case Elizabeth woke and a miracle happened and she could suddenly understand all the private and complex things we spoke about.

I said, 'Go to sleep now, Georgie, and if you want my advice, try not to dwell on the past. Let's just be glad Sassy collected Elizabeth in time, before anybody got hold of her.'

Georgie agreed I was probably right. I fell asleep knowing that I was mature and supportive to those more vulnerable than myself.

Elysian Fields was just as disagreeable in the morning as it had seemed late at night. It was also nearly as dark. The latticed windows were so small and the ancient ceilings so low that, even by midday, it seemed like a November evening. The entry of light was further blocked by the uneven thatched roof which hung down in wispy tatters rather like Daniel's acne-concealing forelock. This thatch was alive with scrabblings and scufflings.

'Reed thatch,' Sarsaparilla said, after I'd observed between chattering teeth, that if this was heaven, it was unexpectedly chilly, 'is one of the most ecologically-sound insulating materials available. Cool in summer, warm in winter.'

I said petulantly, 'Surely for an insulating material to be effective, there should be some interior heat worth retaining.'

The lack of central heating, the mean poky windows, the unkempt thatch like a schoolboy itching with headlice, was supposed to endow the sprawling building with charming rustic simplicity. Unfortunately, none of us (apart from Sarsaparilla) were sophisticated enough to recognize rustic charm when we met it close up.

'Eeergh,' said Georgie. 'This place is just gross!' She wasn't normally fastidious. Her hormones must have started swishing, making her aware that cleanliness could be on a par with godliness.

'Sssseergh!' Edwina agreed.

Elizabeth beamed amicably. 'Chisps,' she said hopefully.

'How can we stay here?' Georgie complained. 'It's unsanitary.'

The detritus of many decades of human and animal habitation had gathered in the corners like low-level historical display centres. Bits and pieces of unidentifiable grey matter, broken clothes pegs, bottle tops, fluff, old hair, small whitish bones. And trails of tiny black things, on the floors, on the kitchen bench, on the musty quilts that covered the beds. I thought they might be fleas. This could be loads more fun than headlice because we could trap them, and train them, and have our own flea circus. But they didn't jump, not even when I prodded them with a twig.

'Course they're not fleas,' said Georgie. 'They're raisin pips.'

They were particularly thick in the larder which was where Sarsaparilla had told us to stack the food supplies. I looked for the fridge to put away the fresh stuff but couldn't find it.

'Little duckling, *nobody* had a fridge when your grandmother was growing up!' Sarsaparilla said. 'Two thirds of the people on earth still don't have fridges. Meanwhile, the western world has far too many. They're clogging up acres and acres of grazing land.'

I said, 'What's the point in showing solidarity with the fridgeless peoples of the world when nobody knows we're doing it? It's just an empty gesture.'

Georgie said, 'And why aren't there any carpets or comfy chairs?'

'Fridges, ottomans, Persian rugs, my pampered petkin, may well be provided in the ashrams of Samarkand but are not what we expect to find in this one,' said Sarsaparilla with a gracious smile. 'We are going to learn to live as ascetically as Franciscan monks so we can concentrate on the higher realms of existence.'

She handed Georgie a birch broom and, unmoved by the grimace of protest, she waddled off to inspect the yard where, she hinted, we'd soon see happy hens clucking and fat ducks waddling. For the time being the yard was full of vigorous thistles.

In collectively surly mood, we started the cleaning. It was a hard task. The rubber gloves had sneaky holes in them. The water was cold. We had no detergents, nicely smelling of lime or pine or peach blossom, for powerful grease-busters are weapons which threaten not only the dirt and germs but also the rivers and waterways.

The trail of little black pips went sneaking across a wooden draining board and onto a bar of cracked yellow soap which was marked with tiny scratches.

Professor Daniel, the Judged of God, shook his wise head. 'Droppings. Definitely.' He picked one up and rubbed it between two fingers. 'Rodents. Poor things. It's not fair, is it? They got here first. I expect they want to be left alone to get on with their lives and then we all turn up to ruin their peace.'

I didn't realize till weeks later that Daniel was not so much expressing solidarity with the rodents as his own desire for solitude. He should never have been part of a large family of argumentative females who were being made to live like Franciscan monks. He was even more unsuited to it than the rest of us.

Georgie said, 'Mr Churchill's a type of rodent. But these aren't a bit like his poos.'

I said, 'I don't know how *you'd* know. *You* never clean him out.'

'Yes I do.'

'No you don't. When was the last time? Go on, give me a date. Bet you can't even *remember* the last time.'

If I was so fond of Georgie, why did I get into arguments with her? It was weird. Perhaps it was the hormones.

Sarsaparilla claimed that love and hate were so close to each other they were the same emotion, the yin and yang, the heads and tails, the two sides of the same coin, the horse and cart which, without each other, were less than half their worth. Back then, in the days before I grew up, I didn't know what she was on about.

'I've done it *loads of times*!' Georgie yelled, flinging the broom on the floor. 'His are brown and squishy. You don't need to be a zoo keeper to tell the difference! Any fool can see it.'

I gazed at Georgie, trying to be objective although I'm not normally an objective sort of person (according to Miss Phillp). I saw how pretty she was, far prettier than Edwina or Tilly, let alone me. (And definitely prettier than Elizabeth, who had a somewhat odd face, like a dear adorable pumpkin.) Georgie's hair curling like wavy seaweed, her cocoa-brown eyes, her warm-as-toast skin, her white teeth, her smile (when she chose to smile, though now she was scowling) all added up to make her just the kind of girl you'd want to be best friends with if you saw her across the playground.

I thought, just supposing we weren't here in the middle of an angry discussion about the state of hygiene of Mr Churchill's cage, but were back living our former lifestyle. Come September, she'd join us at secondary school. Nobody would laugh at her like they laughed at me. Nor bully her as they bullied Daniel. Everybody would admire her. On the first day of term, they'd crowd round, eager to be her best friend. I'd be so proud. When they found out she was my sister, they'd want to be friends with me too. Even if they said, 'She's not your real sister. She's only a foster sister and that doesn't last for ever,' I wouldn't have minded.

But we weren't then. We were now, starting our new life. And all we could do was bicker. If only I believed in praying as Sarsaparilla's late departed mother had, then I'd pray that I could be a real sister to Georgie. If only I knew what real sisters did.

I had an idea. I got it from Cinderella. I knew it was important not to be like *her* sisters. So, reluctantly, I bent down and picked up the broom. It was a morally strong thing for a feeble, undistinguished person like me to accomplish.

'Hey, Georgie,' I said, 'I'll finish in here. You go and have some fun outside.'

Sarsaparilla was right. Love did breed more love because then Daniel picked up a tin bucket and said gruffly, 'S'pose I might as well help wash this stupid floor.' At that, Georgie, who was halfway out of the door with Tilly and Elizabeth, came back in, picked up a rag and started polishing the fly-spotted window over the sink.

'Might as well all do it together,' she muttered. So then Edwina, who'd been getting in everybody's way kicking a pebble round the kitchen as if she thought it was a football ground, decided that sweeping cobwebs off the beams would be a heap more fun.

Thus, for forty minutes we were a contented and united flock.

How My Chalet Socks Got Eaten

Sarsaparilla was away, rattling about in the sheds, chicken houses, and outhouses for hours. When she came in, she scarcely registered our existence, nor our achievements in domesticity. She went thumping upstairs humming to herself with an armful of coloured cotton bedspreads which Mr Singh had thrown out.

I wondered how life might be different if I had a parent with a more structured and consistent approach to the task. Not that Sarsaparilla saw it as a task. For her, it was a joyous life-calling which required no more than offering us PLF (Practical Life Freedoms), plus an abundance of EMA (enduring maternal attention). 'The big L,' she often said. 'No more. No less. That's what the developing soul needs. With enough love, no child can ever go wrong.'

But was she over-simplifying the principles of childcare? I wiped Edwina's nose and resolved that if I ever had to become a mother, I'd have only one child at a time. And I'd borrow a book from the library which would explain in detail, preferably with diagrams, how to care for that child. I would not, however, have the father of the child living in the establishment because, as Sarsaparilla warned, 'Men always disappoint you and even when they aren't doing that, they clutter up the happy home.' (This theory didn't, apparently, apply to the Judged of God, perhaps because he was still too young to be considered a man.)

I said, trying to make light of Sarsaparilla's wilful neglect, ''Spect she's going to make herself a new country-style dress.'

Edwina said she thought Sarsaparilla had gone up to make a pair of pretty curtains for our bedroom to help keep out the draughts. 'Sssosss we'll be warm and sssnug.'

This was an unusually astute guess on Edwina's part since a woman who made dresses out of curtains, was quite likely to make curtains out of bedspreads. The home-maker was briefly viewed again carrying cushions, candlesticks, empty jam jars and a wooden plank, whereupon Daniel said he was quite certain she was creating herself personal space.

'A snug or an office or a bolt-hole. Because no sane adult likes being with their children *all* the time.'

Sarsaparilla reappeared in our midst round about tea-time, looking self-satisfied rather than maternal or holy. None of the girls' guesses were correct. Not a prayer space. Not a cosy maternal chamber where we could gather round her on wet afternoons and listen to stories. Daniel's guess was nearly right. The attic was going to be for her use alone.

'It's my new studio, pets. The purity of light up there is quite superb. The creative rays of heaven will beam down upon my works. And they shall be good.'

'You mean,' I said, surprised, 'you're going to go back

to being an *artist*?' I couldn't remember seeing her touch a paintbrush in months.

'This rural ambience demands it. Never have I felt so inspired. The ethereal atmosphere is too good to be true. Though it's never, ''Go back''. Always, ''Go forward''.'

Her rural enthusiasm wasn't even dented when Daniel told her about the infestation of rodents and that the feral cats had fleas.

'Why, my treasures! That's thrilling beyond measure! The creatures of the wild will share in the tranquil joy of our community.'

Even though Sarsaparilla hadn't put up any curtains for us, the second night we were better prepared for the cold if not for the rodents. Georgie went to bed in all her clothes, including her duffle jacket, gloves, and a scarf. So did I. Except for my best socks which I carefully hung from the metal bed-rail.

Edwina said, 'Jewellssss, s'you exssspessting Sssanta?'

'Course not. Can't you see? I'm airing my socks.'

'S'what for?'

'What d'you think? So they won't get smelly.'

'You ssshould wassssh them.'

'You *know* I never wash them.'

That wasn't a risk I'd ever take. They were my special Swiss *après-ski chaussettes*, red with white snowflakes which, Daniel had been kind enough to inform me on the day in late January when they arrived by post, were supposed to be worn when relaxing in an Alpine chalet in front of a roaring fire drinking hot chocolate with cinnamon. How Daniel thought I'd believe he knew anything about *après-ski* I'd no idea. He was making it up. He'd travelled to snow-capped mountains the same amount as I had.

The man called Richard, who lived so far away that I'd had to write him on a separate sheet of paper for

Mrs Jeans, sent the socks as a Christmas present in an exciting parcel stuck with Japanese stamps. *Cosy toes for my Julia, love Daddy* said the card. I didn't like the man who signed himself Daddy. But I loved the luxury socks. No one else in the family had anything like them.

As I lay shivering in the big cold bed when I should have been in an Alpine chalet, I heard a scratching. Edwina and Tilly were breathing quietly on either side of me so it wasn't them.

'Georgie?' I whispered. 'You there?'

'Course I am, stupid.' She was in the other big bed, sharing with Elizabeth. We'd drawn lots. She'd won the best of it. Elizabeth, though larger than Tilly and Edwina put together, didn't fidget all night long like Edwina, and never ever wet the bed like Tilly.

'Can you hear it?' I whispered.

'Hear what?'

'That scritchy scratchy sound?'

'Yes. Sounds like feet walking.'

'Feet!'

'Hm. Could be. Probably with dirty scaly claws. And a hairy grey body. And a long scaly tail. Hang on a tick. Not sure it's feet. Sounds more like teeth. Chomping. Long yellow fangs.'

I whispered, 'It's getting nearer.' I could feel the pitter-patter movement across my bed. I froze with terror. According to our knowledgeable rodent informant, not only do rats eat lambs, birds, and young humans in their cots, but also transport bubonic plague and other vile lethal diseases.

I heard Georgie strike a match, then give a loud squawk of surprise.

'Oh look, Jewells, look. Isn't he a dear little *sweetie-pie*!' She was sitting up and pointing at the creature on my bed. Not a rat but a very small mouse clutching my Swiss

53

socks in its delicate hands and chewing its way through them with his busy little gnashers.

'Poor ickle fingy,' said Georgie. 'He's ever so hungry-wungry.'

I kicked my feet about.

'Oh, Jewells, don't!'

The mouse glanced up, stared at me with huge glistening eyes, then scuttled away into the shadows.

'Jewells, you horrid thing. You've frightened it off.'

I felt like a nitwit for having been scared of something so small. 'I wish you wouldn't talk in that stupid way!' I snapped at Georgie. 'And I jolly well hope those cats come back indoors and get on with the exterminator work they're supposed to do.'

'Exterminator?' repeated Georgie. 'What do you mean?' She wasn't laughing at me any more.

'I mean ridding our world of unwanted and disease-carrying vermin.'

'You want the kitties to kill that poor little mouse?'

'Yes I do, and then *eat* it! Scrunch, scrunch. Eat all of the mice. That'd stop them destroying people's personal possessions which come from their fathers on the other side of the world.'

'But that's horrible,' Georgie gasped.

'Whoever told you life would be easy? This is what life in the raw is all about, the power struggle of savage beast against savage woman.'

Georgie began to hiccup, then to sniff, finally to weep copiously. She woke Edwina who began to cry too which woke Elizabeth. Her crying woke Tilly. None of them had a clue what they were supposed to be sad about. Between sobs, Georgie told them and sisterly empathy linked them.

'It's all Jewells's fault!' Georgie wailed.

Gasp. Sob. Sniff.

'She wants all the ickle mousies killed off.'

Sniff. Gasp. Wail.

Edwina wailed, 'Ssshe'sss worsssse than a multiple murderesss!'

How could I have upset all my dear sisters at once? 'I didn't mean it, Edwina. Really I didn't. Please don't be upset. I want the dear little mice to stay. I love them.' I couldn't help crying too, though my tears were as much about the dark and the cold and the strangeness of this place.

Five cherubs wailing, howling, sniffing, sobbing. What a din. Sarsaparilla came flying down from her eyrie in the attic, a big white angel with billowing nightie wings.

'There, there, my little chou-chous,' she crooned, enfolding us in her big embrace. 'No, of course the kittens won't hurt the mice. They're all friends of St Francis. They all want to live in perfect harmony.'

The strange thing was that she was almost right. The cats never killed a single mouse because they never came indoors again despite Edwina's attempts to lure them with dabs of butter and saucers of sour milk. The tabby mother and three of her young ran off into the woods. The remaining kittens set up home in the potting-shed.

As for my quality socks, now ruined, Georgie suggested I write to my father explaining the disaster and ask him to send me a new pair.

'You know he's loaded,' she said. 'He can easily afford it.' That's why he and Sarsaparilla had fallen out. Their value systems were too divergent.

'No way,' I said. 'Even if he sent me a hundred pairs of socks, I don't ever want to have anything to do with him.'

And at the time I almost believed it.

How I Listened to a Lot of Hot Air

'Earth, air, water, and fire, my precious honeypots,' Sarsaparilla said. 'Repeat and memorize these four essentials.'

Of the four, fire would be our downfall and change the direction of our lives. Back then, none of us had a clue how fire was made.

We needed to know. It was so cold that Sarsaparilla wore a dusty blanket wrapped round her shoulders. She looked like a peasant shuffling about on a frozen steppe. But however cold she may have been inside, she was still smiling warmly as she explained about the elements which were apparently the components of all life.

'And thus, my chitterlings, henceforth, we take them to be our guiding principles.' She looked so enthusiastic and her eyes shone so brightly, that of course I wanted to believe her. I needed a parent I could trust, a mother who knew what she was doing, an adult who would guide me, lead the way, make sense of a variously disrupted life.

Not Daniel though. Of course he didn't agree with her. He always knew better than everybody.

'Four?' he said frostily. 'Whadyou mean *four*? What you talking about? Of course there's more than four elements which make up life. There's a hundred and five.'

He began to rattle off their names in alphabetical order.

'Actinium, aluminium, americium, antimony, argon, arsenic, astatine, barium, berkelium, beryllium, bismuth, boron, bromine, cadmium, caesium, calcium, californium, carbon, cerium, chlorine, chromium, cobalt, copper, curium, dysprosium, einsteinium, erbium, europium, fermium, fluorine, francium, gadolinium, gallium, germanium, gold, hafnium, hahnium, helium, holmium, hydrogen, indium.'

'Whassat? Whasss he on about?' said Edwina.

'Ssh. Let him finish. It's funny,' I said. I'd heard him do it before. It was impressive, like listening to a mystical, semi-comprehensible poem.

'Iodine, iridium, iron, krypton, lanthanum,' Daniel went on, as unstoppable as a runaway kitten.

'Lawrencium, lead, lithium, lutetium, magnesium, manganese, mendelevium, mercury, molybdenum, neodymium, neon, neptunium, nickel, niobium, nitrogen, nobelium, osmium, oxygen, palladium, phosphorus, platinum, plutonium, polonium, potassium, praseodymium, promethium, protactinium, radium, radon, rhenium, rhodium, rubidium, ruthenium, rutherfordium, samarium, scandium, selenium, silicon, silver, sodium, strontium, sulphur, tantalum, technetium, tellurium, terbium, thallium, thorium, thulium, tin, titanium, tungsten, uranium, vanadium.'

Daniel paused for breath.

'Xenon, ytterbium, yttrium, zinc, zirconium,' he finished in a rush.

Blanket Woman blinked, smiled, shook her head as if in despair at Daniel's great wisdom.

'And that's not counting the atmospheric elements like winds and storms,' Daniel suddenly remembered. 'Moreover, should more positive evidence be necessary, I shall now give you the atomic value of each of the chemical elements, in ascending scale, starting with hydrogen which is in first place.'

'Whassat? Whassee on about now?' said Edwina. 'I don't gettit.'

I said, 'The learned brother speaks with the authority of science. Blanket Woman conveys information in an artistic manner.'

'Tosh manner, more like,' said Daniel. 'The medieval scholars were talking *philosophically*, not literally. They didn't *understand* so much about *science*, did they? They said there were *four* elements because they hadn't discovered the full range.'

'Highly favoured first-born son,' said Sarsaparilla, in a tone edging on the argumentative, 'certain facts retain their eternal truth throughout the aeons of time, and to these we must adhere.'

'Pah,' said Daniel.

'*Favoured* son?' gasped Georgie. Daniel had been centre of attention for too long.

'Lighten up, it's just her joke,' I said calmingly. 'He's the *only* son. So there's no competition.'

'What about *me*?' said Georgie.

'You're not a son,' I said reasonably. 'You could be her most highly favoured daughter if it's important to you. I don't mind. Don't suppose Elizabeth does either. Or Tilly.'

But Edwina minded. A lot. '*S'ssme*!' she shouted. '*I'ss* mossst favoured daughter.'

'Course you aren't,' said Georgie, giving her a biff. 'You're just a lispy nuisance.'

I wondered, Did they always argue or was this part of the ashram effect?

I said, 'Daniel doesn't even want to be favourite son.'

He said, 'The trouble with you, Sassy, is you always over-simplify things. It doesn't help.'

'That's correct, my petkins,' she said. 'The purity of love is always simple,' and with a mischievous grin, she sneaked an unexpected kiss on his acned forehead.

Now *that*, I reckoned, really was an indication of maternal affection. If ever I had children, I'd never be able to kiss them when they're spotty.

'Simplifying life is why we're here. So that we can unleash from within ourselves those hidden energies for cosmic creativity and the transformation of our lives to total purity.'

Daniel strode out of the kitchen slamming the door behind him.

'Sss'bad mannersss ssslamming doorsss,' said Miss Goody-Two-Shoes.

I thought, even though I wasn't often a thoughtful person, What a pain that child could be.

The shudder of the door woke Mr Churchill in his cage on the windowsill. He began to scrabble though it wasn't his normal time of day for being awake. He looked miserable, his shoulders hunched, his fur clumpy. I don't know why I ever wished I were a hamster. I was beginning to wish I wasn't me and I wasn't here. I wished I was in a warm safe classroom finding out about Henry's wives.

'Such a dear boy,' said Blanket Woman. 'Even when he's riding on his high horse.' (She meant Daniel, not Mr Churchill.) 'He's got a heart of gold inside.'

'Which is currently invisible,' I grumbled.

'I expect he's gone to search for firewood.' As usual, Sarsaparilla looking on the bright side.

But she sensed, with her uncanny intuitive skill, that we were down in the dumps about Elysian Fields so she didn't go back up to her studio to mess around with her quotidian art. Instead, she stayed in the kitchen, unwrapped herself from the blanket, and did something fantastic, something which many children may take for granted but not us.

For the first time in many months, Sarsaparilla prepared a meal. All by herself. *Without any help.*

How We Had Food
for Thought

Much effort went into the artistic decoration of the kitchen. It was soon festooned with loops of ivy and dried hops stretching from wall to wall like Christmas paper-chains. Sarsaparilla set the table for her festive banquet with posies of ferns, thistles, and dandelions in jam jars, and laid a flickering stream of lighted candles in bottles down the centre.

Less effort was expended on food preparation.

The menu was a familiar one. Potatoes. Carrots. Onions. Pot of tea with long-life milk with the curious diesel after-taste which, until we got our own cow/goat we'd have to learn to make friends with.

It was never my personal choice to become a vegetarian (and, unlike Georgie, I didn't weep and wail over furry things being killed) but pick-ups can't be choosers so I was a vegetarian by default even though my favourite form of nutritional intake would always be a packet of chocolate-coated shortcake biscuits for starters, two burgers with large fries, a litre of tomato relish, followed by a couple of jam and cream pastry puffs and enough brightly coloured sugary fizzy drink to swim in.

But when you're really hungry, even a cracked dish piled high with a rocky cairn of steaming boiled potatoes can make your mouth water.

Sarsaparilla set it on the table with a flourish. 'Behold!' she said. 'And marvel at the magnificent South American tuber, king of vegetables.'

She hadn't bothered to peel the potatoes so their limp skins were flapping about like loose grey scabs. Inside, they were so dry and floury it was like eating the white powdery DIY stuff that Feeble John used to use for mending cracks in the bathroom walls. Edwina prodded with her fork, then wrinkled up her nose in disgust. Probably she wasn't a true dyed-in-the-wool vegetarian either. Probably that's why she was so thin. Her body was craving red meat, sausages, fried liver, black pudding, best back bacon, and a couple of roast chicken legs.

'That's right, petal. You dab some lovely butter on,' Sarsaparilla encouraged. 'That'll make them extra tasty.'

As if the simple application of butter could turn a potato into a feast. It wasn't even butter anyway. It was cheapo margarine with the same diesel flavour as the long-life milk.

She'd done a pan of cabbage too, boiled in deep water till it was grey and definitely dead.

'This seaweed stuff's really strange,' said Georgie. 'Is it meant to taste like this?'

'I didn't want to burn it, ducky. There's nothing so bad as burned cabbage, is there?' She hadn't washed the cabbage. I found much grit and a pale earwig on my plate. At least it wasn't wiggling. I didn't complain but I couldn't eat it even though I didn't consider myself to be a true vegetarian.

There was bread too, shaped like a brick.

'And for dessert,' said Sarsaparilla, her voice quivering with affection, 'I've made everybody's favourite strawberry treat!'

Why on earth did I think it'd be that delicious strawberry shortcake like her mum used to bake for us?

It was ordinary red jelly. It was liquid. It hadn't set and it never would. She'd added far too much water for one packet of jelly. It was like scooping up cold soup. We girls humoured her. We pretended it was the nicest dessert we'd ever had. Not Daniel. He was back in one of his hormone-induced male moods.

'True vegetarians don't eat jelly,' he growled. His voice was much lower than usual. He was obviously going through some kind of change, like a worm inside its chrysalis (though I doubted he'd ever emerge as a moth).

Georgie said, 'Why not? It's not meaty. It's all sweet and fruity.'

'True vegetarians know where gelatine comes from.'

'And where's *that*?' Georgie asked in a sulky tone. It would've been better if she hadn't asked anything.

'Boiled-up bovine tendons.'

Daniel had such a talent for putting the dampers on any attempt at family harmony.

'Eergh!' squealed Georgie. 'You're so mean. Why d'you have to tell me? I was enjoying it and now you've really put me off.' She scooped up a spoonful of wet jelly and flicked it towards him. It landed on his forehead blending in with the red spots. He flicked some back. It splatted on her nose. Then it slid down her lip towards her mouth. It looked like she'd been in a playground scuffle and got a biff in the face.

She licked the jelly off with exaggerated slurps of

pleasure to prove how little she cared what it was made from. Then she flicked some back at Daniel. It missed. It hit me instead. I licked it off trying not to give any thought to bovine tendons. I flicked some back at Georgie, then at Edwina. She flicked at Daniel.

He flicked in all directions at everybody. And we ended up having a Grade-A jelly-fight which was far better than any ketchup-fight. Ketchup stings your skin and it's no fun to lick off.

We flicked and we licked till there was no jelly left in the dish but plenty around the kitchen. Tilly had jelly in her hair and her ears. She found a jelly-splat on the stone floor and rolled in it, gurgling merrily.

'Sss'es like a piggy, sss'rolling in mud!' Edwina laughed and joined her on the floor.

The only person who didn't see the funny side was Elizabeth. In her slow-brain way, she was always so well-behaved. She sat on the wooden bench, stubby little hands neatly folded in her lap and she stared. 'Bleeding,' she said plaintively. 'Everybody bleeding.'

'It's not blood, Lizziekins,' I reassured her. 'It's Daniel's brilliant new game.' (I named him as inventor even though it was in fact me.)

'Silly,' said Elizabeth. 'Girls and boys do silly.'

I didn't explain that some games are supposed to be silly. It wasn't worth the effort. She wouldn't have understood, being enclosed inside her double-bubble. I was sad for her though, that she understood so little, that she missed so much of normal family fun. As the jelly-fight drew to its finale, I rushed over to Elizabeth and gave her a sticky hug. She turned and beamed with a smile like moonshine. Even if she couldn't understand the point of jelly-fighting, at least she knew she was loved.

But was love enough for a dearly beloved mystic with a double-wrapped brain?

If I was beginning to suspect that Elizabeth was not an ideal candidate for the ashram way of life, I kept it to myself.

Why We Didn't Go to Dancing Classes

Childhood is an important time for mental exploration and physical experimentation. Everybody knows. And if they don't, they can look it up in a book about childcare.

Children shouldn't slump in front of the telly or crouch before their playstation every evening, not when there are so many fascinating hobbies they can take up. They can learn to play the violin, clarinet, piano, recorder. They can join the swimming club. The football team. Scouts or Guides. St John's Ambulance Brigade. They can locate a drama group and act plays, or a gymnastics team and jump on trampolines. Or play tennis on a green rubber table-top or on grass.

Not us. We didn't join anything, go anywhere, discover any unusual skill. When I have children I'll send them out to a different activity every evening, even if they get wiped out with exhaustion.

When I grow up and write a guidance manual about effective childcare, I shall explain how it is the parents' duty to encourage their youngsters, however reluctant, to try out new activities. This is to get them socialized, to give them a taste of fun so they don't get claustrophobia, cabin fever, go crazy with being in each other's company all day long. My current parent didn't think any of this was necessary.

'Sweetheart-petal, what d'you want to mix with other children for when you've got each other?' she said. 'Just look at yourselves! You're such a *wonderful* team, all of you pulling together like this. I'm so proud of you!'

'What if we need to expand our horizons?'

'Then you're spoiled for choice when you've this beautiful countryside all around.'

'What if we need friends?'

'You've the trees for company.'

First, make friends with the darkness. Now make friends with the trees.

Round the back of Elysian Fields it was all nettles, then brambles, then trees. Beyond them lay wide brown fields as far as you could see. If you sneaked up to Sarsaparilla's studio and craned your neck through the skylight, you could just make out the top of a tower. But it was a long way off.

'As pale as a long-lost phantom prince,' said Georgie dreamily. 'As distant as a long-lost hope.'

Daniel said flatly, 'That's a church. In the next village.'

I said, 'How do *you* know? You got X-ray vision or a telescope?'

'No. But I've got a map,' he said. 'Maps tell you where you are.'

As the third night closed in around us, and the trees started to ache and groan, and the creatures in the thatch started to scrabble, and beetles in rafters to gnaw, it felt as if we were zillions of miles from all other human habitation.

'Nobody'll *ever* know where we are,' Georgie said. 'Even if they search. It's like we're sleeping princesses lost in the briars.'

'Except for Daniel,' I sniggered. 'He'll never make it as a lost princess.'

Daniel growled in his new-style, randomly deep, man's voice.

To be lost in the briars was precisely how Sarsaparilla wanted it so that the terrible thing that happened to little Rupert, taken away by a woman in a taxi with all his sad possessions stuffed in a black bin-liner, would not happen to us.

'That baby boy,' she said with a misty look clouding her yellowish eyeballs. 'I loved him so much. How often do I wonder what'll become of him without a full family's love to protect him?'

So, instead of taking up interesting hobbies, we stayed close by her as a family unit, and had to go on learning from our weird wise mother about the four fantastic elements.

'The air that governs our life is the soft southerly wind, the zephyrs wafting from the Azores to inspire our hearts with contentment and inner stillness.'

'Blah blah,' Georgie muttered.

Could ever a soft wind prevent children's discontent?

'No, Georgie, I'm sure she's right,' I said. 'When spring comes.'

As if spring ever would come to this fool's paradise. The air currently governing our life was the rapier draught slicing up through the cracks in the floor, the breezes knifing down through the gap in the thatch, rattling like castanets through the broken window-panes, the mean wind which whistled around the rooftops, the malevolent gusts which howled down the chimneys to puff black soot into our eyes and make them smart.

[Please note that the preceding descriptive paragraph is not my own unaided work. I nicked most of it from one of Daniel's journals that he left behind when he escaped.]

In other seasons, the water of life might have been, as Sarsaparilla claimed, the sweet morning dew gathering like diamonds on the delicate petals of the wild heartsease. As we experienced it, it was condensation gathering in glistening drops on the walls. It was the humid clouds we made when we breathed or yawned or spoke. It was sand-coloured stuff that dribbled from the brass tap over the stone sink in the scullery. It was the rain that fell and fell and fell from the dark winter sky and turned the ground around the house into a swamp.

Sarsaparilla assured us that the earth of our lives was loam, dark and rich as chocolate, which would bring forth the delectable fruits of the earth for our nourishment. For the time being, the earth of life was so closely involved with the water of life that it was a sticky mud clogging our boots, a brownish slurry swishing around the yard, a leafy soup which made the track across our meadow to the lane impassable.

And the fire of life was—? What was it? My brain was foggy. Tilly was teething. It was her back molars. She'd been grizzling all night, keeping us awake more effectively than the noisy mice.

'What's the element of fire supposed to be again, Georgie?'

She couldn't remember either. 'I think it was the dark destructive pool which encompasses all, all, all of something else ever so important only I didn't really understand what she was on about.'·

'Fire,' Daniel interrupted, 'is the active principle in combustion in which substances join chemically with oxygen in air and give out light and heat.' He wasn't quoting from the wisdoms of Sarsaparilla but from his own superior fund of information.

It was no surprise that Daniel proved to be as knowledgeable about the theory of fire as he was about everything. Which is not to say that I blame him for what happened. It wasn't his fault. It wasn't anybody's fault, except perhaps Sarsaparilla's. And she paid the price for her folly of romanticism.

'The earliest evidence,' said Daniel, 'for deliberate and planned use of controlled fire, as distinct from spontaneously igniting forest fires, or conflagration caused by electric storms, or sparks elicited by friction, dates from Peking man, five hundred thousand years ago.'

I said, 'Yeah, OK. But how d'you *do* it?' Because when you've lived an ordinary urban life with radiators and electricity you've had no practical experience beyond the little pastel candles on a birthday cake.

Georgie said. 'How many noughts?'

Daniel said, 'What d'you mean?'

'How many noughts is there in five hundred thousand?'

Daniel said, 'Five.'

I said, 'Stop quibbling about how long ago it was and let's just get on and *do* it.'

Practical Experiments
with Fire

'You need paper. Paper ignites at the relatively low temperature of four hundred and fifty-seven degrees Fahrenheit.'

Daniel knew the theory, or some of it. But successful fire-lighting, however straightforwardly scientific it may seem, is an operation requiring more than theoretical knowledge. It needs patience and sustained practice.

The hearth squatted sullenly at one end of the kitchen. It demanded a type of love and attention that we didn't yet understand. At least we had matches. A box with a picture of a swan on the lid sat cosily in Tilly's chubby fist.

'Duck, duck, quack, quack,' she said, kissing the swan with her fat lips.

'Get them off her!' ordered Daniel. 'That's phosphorous. P. Atomic number 15 in the table of chemical elements. And poisonous.'

Tilly prised the box open. She saw how each match had a pink bobble-top like a dolly's lolly.

Daniel grabbed the box just before she popped a matchstick in her mouth. Tilly screamed. I gathered her up and tried to cuddle her.

'It's her teeth, hurting her,' I said.

'No it's not,' said Georgie. 'It's Daniel stealing her box. It's the only toy she's got.'

I said, 'Take her outside then, Georgie, there's an angel, while Daniel and I get the fire going.' I made it sound so easy.

'It's raining,' said Georgie.

I said, 'Go and play in the big barn then. Or look for the kittens. Surely a big intelligent girl like you can entertain a tiny two year old for a short time. We won't be long.'

But even Daniel with his superior knowledge found it frustratingly difficult to get started. He used up over half the box of Swan vestas and still no lasting fire. I gave useful encouragement.

'If primitive Peking people sitting in their cold cave all those years ago managed to work it out, old bean,' I said, as affectionately brisk as a junior Sarsaparilla, 'I'm sure we can. And they didn't even have matches.'

'They'd have used friction,' Daniel mumbled glumly. 'But that takes ages.'

So did our method. The reasons for recurring failure were various. The wood that Daniel had collected was so damp that it had moss and slimy fungal things growing on it. The chimney was cold. The wind was in the wrong direction. We had too many down-draughts and not enough up-draughts. We had no small dry twigs.

'It's just hopeless,' I said. 'We might as well give up now.'

Our fires burned up suddenly, then went out. Or they never even started. Or they seemed to be out, yet filled the kitchen with smoke so we had to rush for the door and sit outside with streaming eyes. We lay on the floor and puffed, we stood up and fanned with a saucepan lid. We failed and tried again and failed once more. Until, miraculously, suddenly, we found we'd created our first fire, with real flickering flames and a red glowing heart.

We stood back to admire it. I was surprised how well we'd worked together. Bonding like sister to brother. Perhaps I even almost loved him.

'Well done us,' I said and gave him a hug.

Daniel smirked and scratched the back of his head. 'Hmph,' he said and busied himself breaking up more twigs into little pieces.

It was a while before we'd perfected our skill enough to pass it on to Georgie and Edwina.

'They need to know,' I said. 'Otherwise it's always going to be up to us, isn't it?'

He agreed. 'And if one of us wasn't here, then everybody'd freeze to death.'

'What d'you mean?'

'You know what freeze means, don't you? And death. Put them together. And you get a row of frozen corpses.'

'No, I meant, "not here"?'

He shrugged. 'If one of us had to go away. For whatever reason.'

How to Lay and Light
a Fire Correctly

I said, 'Now listen carefully. First you clean the grate. If you leave it piled up with all that old ash, the air can't get in.'

'Oxygen,' Daniel corrected. 'Fire needs oxygen. Without oxygen, it pines and dies.'

Like me, who needed chips and pizzas and clementines and jam puffs and Belgian chocolate biscuits.

'Also, do not remove *all* the ash. Leave enough to make a good bed.'

'Bed?' said Georgie.

I said, 'Like a futon. For the fire to sit on, to make it comfy.'

Daniel scowled disapprovingly. 'You're getting to sound like Sarsaparilla, over-simplifying things.'

'Then you need old newspaper, dry sticks, dry leaves, bits of straw or grass.'

'Kindling,' Daniel corrected me. 'Why don't you use the proper terms?'

'Because then they won't have a clue what we're on about,' I said. 'Always remember to place your sticks crossways or in a wigwam, but not in a tidy pile. Take care to make no sudden movements or you stir up the ash.'

Wood ash is as fine as snow and, like snow, it drifts all over the place. Sometimes it landed in the milk and made it speckled. But Daniel said, 'That won't hurt us. French people even roll their cheese in it.'

Wood ash is also like love. That gets everywhere, too, and after a while you can't even tell it's there.

'The efficient fire-master uses a single match. When striking, draw away from your body, having first closed the box so there is no danger of a spark landing on the phosphorous.'

'Once your fire has a secure heart you can burn anything on it.'

'Except feathers,' Daniel interrupted. 'On no account try to burn feathers.'

He and I had unwisely set fire to a deceased pigeon which tumbled down the chimney with a lot of soot. The desiccated corpse burned well but the smell of singeing feathers was worse than any smells that Tilly could make and it put everybody off their porridge.

Edwina, on her first lesson, threw a sheet of newspaper into the grate. Then, from some distance because she was so nervous she might scorch her fingers, tossed in a lighted match. The match hit the back wall of the hearth, then, still aflame, bounced out of the grate and onto the brick floor where it flared for a second before going out.

'You have to scrumple up the paper first, Edwina,' I explained. 'The scrumpling's important.'

'To create micro-pockets and channels through which draughts can run, transporting oxygen,' said Daniel.

Edwina pouted. Fed up with being instructed, she deliberately threw another flat, unscrumpled sheet of paper into the grate before walking away. 'Ssstupid. Little ssschildren ssshouldn't do fire. You're not making Elisssabesss do fire. Sso you can't make me.'

'Don't you *want* to learn things and improve yourself?'

An unexpected gust sucked her flat sheet of paper up the chimney. Like a letter destined for Santa, it disappeared from sight.

Several moments later it reappeared, drifting gently downwards, flames curling prettily round the edges. It had reached some soot smouldering further up the chimney.

The flaming paper settled on Edwina's badly-arranged twigs and set them alight without any more intervention from any of us.

Fire is one of the unpredictable elements, as we were to discover.

So was that smouldering soot a warning? Was it informing us that chimneys should be swept? Daniel thought so. He told Sarsaparilla.

'Why, treasurekins, you old-fashioned romantic!' She tousled his hair before he had a chance to duck out of the way. 'There *are* no more chimney-sweeps! And we wouldn't want there to be, would we, sweetheart? Such a barbaric practice, sending little orphans with ropes round their ankles up into the dark.'

Put like that, you could see she was right. So the chimney remained unswept.

Elemental Living

There's a Greek word which I found in one of the secret journals that Daniel left behind. Hubris. It means the pride that comes before the fall.

Daniel and I became exceptionally good at fire. We knew we were good and we marvelled at our own brilliance. We were guilty of hubris.

How we nurtured that fire! When it sulked, we coaxed it to good humour. When it was peckish, we fed it choice titbits.

We discovered how, at dawn, the dead ash still held a hidden memory of the previous day's warmth. It could be stirred skilfully with a thin dry stalk to seek out and uncover the memory. Then, with soft baby breaths, the corpse of the dead fire could be urged to live without the use of a single match.

I told Daniel that since we were so good at dealing with this element, we'd soon be able to get going on the other three.

'Specially earth. I'm really looking forward to when we start growing things, start eating the fruits of our labour.'

He grunted. Was he like a Greek oracle? Could he see it was never going to happen? I said, 'OK, so I know that we probably won't produce an abundance of strawberries or cherries or peaches at first, but even when we grow our own radishes or cress, it'll be an achievement, won't it?'

Daniel said, 'Earth would be a less immediately satisfying element to work with than fire. It'd require intense application and long-term vision.' Note the 'would' not 'will'. He'd been thinking about it. As I later discovered, he'd been writing about it too.

'Horticulture. The seven stages of making a garden. One. Clear it. Two. Dig it. Three. Plant it. Four. Tend it. Five. Feed it. Six. Harvest. Seven. Repeat all over again.'

So far, we'd barely reached stage one. Working outside was so cold and so wet. But with fire, we were supreme masters. That fire was more than a heap of burning wood. It became our child and our parent. All day we looked after it so that it would be there for us in the evening when we pulled over the benches and gathered round and stared into the flames. The kittens, bedraggled from the lashing rain, crept in to dry out their fur. Mr Churchill peddled happily round his exercise wheel. And we waited for Sarsaparilla to come down to join the family circle, to be our epicentre.

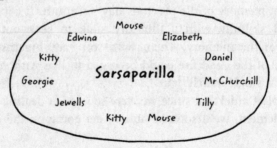

We needed her to tell us bedtime stories like she used to. Tales about us which explained where we'd each come from, tales which may or may not have been true. It didn't matter. With the power of her presence, by the mesmerism of her invention, she knew how to hold us together, how to make each of us know how much we were valued.

'For it has been proved through irrefutable sociological research,' she once told me, 'that it is around the contented mother that the secure family thrives.'

But now she wasn't here for us to thrive around. It was the fault of her art, taking her in new directions. She had little time for anything else. She was following the magnetic pull of a newly awakened vision which was, apparently, leading her on to a higher plane.

Wrapped in her blanket against the wind, Art Woman foraged in the woods collecting outdoor rubbish. 'Mother Nature's Bounty' she called it. Moss and straw, seed-pods and leaves, bits of bright orange binder-twine she found in the hedgerows.

Instead of using paint, she scraped up handfuls of mud to mix with water, dark and slimy, wriggling with little red worms, which she ladled out of the wooden rain-collecting butt in the yard.

'The good earth of life, the water of life, the truest colour pigments obtainable,' she enthused. 'Through their use, I reverence the earth.'

What was she going to do with it all? What would it mean?

'This will be a distillation of the contradictions of life itself,' she explained, which didn't make it any clearer to me, perhaps because I've never been a very creative person. (So Miss Phillp told me.)

I was elbow-deep in potato peel at the sink when Sarsaparilla roared down the stairs to me to come at once. I had work to do. I took no notice. But she went on calling.

'Jewells, lovey! Jewells! *Do* come up and see what I've been doing today!' she yelled excitedly. 'Bring Tilly and Elizabeth too! They'll be fascinated.'

Tilly's bad nights with her sore gums were making her difficult and demanding. She was becoming clingy, wanting to be carried everywhere, even holding out her chubby little arms to Edwina who was practically the same size. Now she pulled my hair and drummed her little feet against my shins in stubborn protest. She had no wish to be taken upstairs to admire Sassy's incomprehensibly brown and mossy art.

But I hated hurting Sarsaparilla's feelings.

'Sassy,' I called. 'Can't bring Tilly up. It's not safe. The steps are too wobbly.' There were also holes in the floor into which she might fall, and no handrail so she might slip over the edge.

'Then bring Elizabeth, I'd love to get her reaction.'

But Elizabeth wasn't interested either.

'Busy,' she said with a broad smile, and refused to budge from her place on the bench beside the hearth. 'Busy busy bee.'

Busy? Elizabeth? She never lifted a finger. She didn't even have to dress herself. We saw to her every need.

I went up on my own to Sarsaparilla's studio.

'Welcome, welcome!' she said as if I were some honoured art dealer. 'I'm working on the power of trees. They've been speaking to me. Can you see how I'm beginning to capture their sustaining power?'

The pictures were getting bigger and darker. But I still didn't understand what they were meant to be saying. So I said, 'Very nice, Sassy.'

She looked pleased.

I said, 'Would you like me to bring you up some tea? Or will you come down?' She followed me down.

Elizabeth's face brightened when she saw her. Tilly's

too. They'd been missing her. Tilly reached out her arms for a cuddle. But elusive Art Woman hadn't come down to join us at the table for potatoes, onions, and cabbage.

'Sycamore seeds!' she said.

She started to rifle through the box of kindling that Daniel and I had collected earlier that day as feverishly as Mr Churchill scrabbling through the litter in his cage searching out a favourite grain.

Daniel stared, mouth agape. I gave him a reassuring shake of my head.

'It's all right,' I mouthed. 'It's for the power of the trees.'

What to us was a box of useful kindling drying out beside the fire was, to the artist, a new source of material, conveniently stored indoors. With intense concentration, she selected a handful of seed pods and waddled back up to the attic.

Why did we keep our kindling in a cardboard box so close to the fire? What a stupid place. Were we completely daft? A rogue spark could spring out at any moment and set the whole boxful alight as quick as a wink.

Of course, I can see it clearly now because I've grown up such a lot. Everybody says so. But I didn't know it then. None of us did. Some people say Sarsaparilla ought to have known. But how could she? She was an artist. They're not supposed to be responsible.

When Things Began
to Fall Apart

It was only small things at first. Like, Georgie couldn't find any dry wood. So she fed the fire with a wobbly chair-leg, a loose floorboard, and half a broken window-shutter. Top marks for lateral-thinking, you might think. But Daniel didn't. He was seething.

'Why d'you think Jewells and I get up at dawn and go out in the rain and collect dead branches and break them up into nice easy lengths and stack them by the door? *Why*, Georgie? We do it to save *you* trouble and so *you* won't have to dismantle our home for firewood. *Geddit?*'

So Georgie sulked for half an hour which was most uncharacteristic.

Two days later, at breakfast, we found a tiny splodge of porridge, the size of a walnut, in each of our bowls.

It was Georgie's doing. She was on porridge duty.

'Hey, what's *this* supposed to be?' I said, tapping the

side of my bowl with the spoon. 'New-style starvation diet? Just because *you* need to lose a bit of weight doesn't mean we *all* have to.' I thought she'd done it deliberately because of the incident of the firewood.

'Sorry,' she said and she looked as though she meant it, specially as she ended up having to sit on the three-legged chair.

She'd made horribly weak tea. It was in one of Sarsaparilla's favourite charity shop collectables. The pot had a cracked spout and no lid so you could see that Georgie had only used one tea-bag for the whole family.

She said, 'I was trying to make them last. There's only six left.'

We were running out of other supplies too. We had a scraping of peanut butter in the bottom of the tub, ten tins of baked beans, eleven packs of the long-life milk that tasted like it was made out of fish oil, and not much else.

Being hungry first thing on a damp morning and yearning for four toasted waffles dripping with maple syrup, and a chocolate milk-shake, when all that's available is a teaspoonful of brown sludgy porridge, can make any person, even a level-headed and reasonable one such as myself, feel ratty.

'You should've checked last night,' I snapped. 'And when you'd *seen* there weren't enough oats for the morning, you should've *done* something about it. Problems don't melt away all by themselves, you know.' I hated myself for sounding like Miss Phillp. I hated being hungry even more.

'But there *wasn't* anything I could've done,' Georgie wailed.

'Then you should've told Sarsaparilla. And do stop snivelling. It's so depressing.'

'You know Sassy hates being disturbed, specially when she's doing that meditation thing.'

Georgie was right. It was increasingly hard to talk to our parent-figure. Failing household supplies had never aroused her interest. Even when she seemed to be with us, she was emotionally absent.

In order to unleash her full creative potential, Sarsaparilla was having to seek out the tap-root of her inner spirituality. This meant sitting very still on one of Mr Singh's bedspreads and staring ahead at her mossy artworks. Searches for inner self required spiritual silence so she didn't answer even when we spoke.

If she wanted to tell us something important, she left us a note.

To Whomsoever is on tea duty: henceforth, honey in tea please, one spoonful. No more white sugar which provides only negative energy and harmful denatured nutrients.

To Whom It May Concern: Mr Churchill. Getting a bit niffy? Time for a clean-out?

Regarding Tilly. How's that potty-training coming along? Any signs of progress?

Tilly made as many puddles on the floor as the kittens. If she lived out of doors it wouldn't have bothered us.

'Honey!' Daniel exploded. 'Where's she think we're going to get *honey* from?'

Georgie would remain on breakfast-duty until the meal was over and it was all cleared up. I said, 'So why not ask her, quite casually, when you take up her morning tray?'

At which, Edwina decided to throw a tantrum. 'Sssnot fair! S'whyss sssshe get tea upssstairsss in bed and not *me*? I want to ssstay in bed and be ssspiritual.'

'Sassy has her breakfast in bed, sweetheart,' I said in what I hoped was my usual mature and reasonable tone, 'because she is our beloved mother and also she is an artist tapping the roots of inner greenness and the world has a duty to take care of its precious artists.'

I did not invent this viewpoint myself. It was something I'd once heard Sarsaparilla say about Ralph. That's why they'd had to separate. His precious talent was, apparently, too fragile to withstand the knocks of everyday life and wasn't getting enough attention from his then-wife.

If anything was to change about the encroaching food shortage, we were going to have to see to it ourselves. I did the first thing. While I was out in the barn looking for the kittens to give them some of the fishoil-flavoured milk in a saucer, I banged my head on something. I looked up and discovered a plaited string of onions hanging from a beam. Most of them had gone soft and were sprouting green tops. But a few looked more or less edible. The onion, according to one of Sarsaparilla's previous nutrition instructions, is excellent for combating arthritis, rheumatism, and gout.

'Pah!' said Daniel. 'The nutritional value of an onion is nil.'

I whined plaintively, 'Well at least I *tried* which is a lot more than some people round here do.'

So he made the next move. He took Edwina on a wooding expedition and they returned not only dragging long branches but their pockets bulging with potatoes. They tipped them out, along with a lot of sand and mud, onto the table.

'We found this potato-clamp,' said Daniel beaming.

'Clamp?' I said.

'Storage heap,' said Daniel. 'On the edge of a field. Covered in straw.'

Edwina was very excited. 'We sssought it wasss a goblinsss' cassstle for climbing onto!' she squeaked with round eyes. 'Sssen we sssaw potatoesss peeking out ssso we helped oursssselvesss!'

I said, shocked, 'Daniel! How could you? That's *stealing*!'

85

Daniel shrugged. 'Not stealing. Requisitioning for redistribution amongst the poor of the land.'

Edwina said, 'We'sss only taken a sss'few. There'sss loadsss sss'left.'

I said, 'You shouldn't go teaching her bad habits.'

This was not yet an emergency. But supposing the situation escalated? What if Daniel started taking all of them out on thieving expeditions? What if someone saw him and he got caught? What if they all got caught except for me because I was too prudish to go stealing? They'd all get sent to detention centres and I'd be left alone with Sarsaparilla for the rest of my life.

I searched urgently for something to write with and something to write on. I found a pen. It was a free one from Oxfam. Sarsaparilla must have been sent it. She gave away loads of money to charities. In return, they sent her name on to other charities who sent her cheap pens. She didn't need any more pens. She needed people to listen to her potty ideas. They should've been sending their pens to the faraway places where there's pen-less, fridge-less kids who want to go to school.

Sarsaparilla was still tapping silently into the roots of her greening power. I wrote my message.

SOS. Urgent!!! Children at risk in this house. Supplies running LOW. Children hungry. Children also in moral danger. Need more milk, need honey, need noodles, need lentils. Need everything.

I shoved it under the studio door.

She responded quickly. She left me a cheerful, brightly painted message on a scrap of old card. *Help yourself* was entwined with decorative vines, suns, rainbow-coloured flower-heads. The card was propped up against her petty-cash toffee-tin. It was stuffed with cash. Perhaps she hadn't been sending so many donations to charity lately.

Georgie and I wrote a shopping list on a strip of newspaper we salvaged from the floor of Mr Churchill's cage. Now all we had to do was lure Sarsaparilla to climb behind the wheel of the camper-van so she could drive us to town. I was excited in anticipation of the other essentials we might persuade her to let us buy. Shampoo? Conditioner? Lip salve? Maybe even a small amount of organic chocolate. Unfortunately, I was quite unaware of another essential element of our lives that had begun to fall apart.

The Faithless Pink
Camper-van

All the way to Leicester and back every week with the
entire Singh dynasty on board. But, for the Greens, the van
couldn't journey beyond a rural backwater without
conking out.

All morning Daniel fiddled around with a spanner and
an oily rag looking mechanically knowing.

'Fan-belt's gone,' he said importantly. Then changed
his mind. 'Spark plugs must be damp.'

I said, 'I didn't know you knew anything about
engines.'

He said, 'Could be the distributor head. Or the universal
alternator.'

I could see through the ruse of the oily rag. I said,
'You don't really know, do you?'

He didn't. 'Engines are very complex. There's a
thousand things it might be.'

So I had to write Sarsaparilla another note explaining the transport situation and hoping she'd have some useful recommendation. After lunch (boiled potatoes, fried onions) she wrote back.

O young lionhearts! Who needs wheels when you've all got legs!

Note the *'you've* all got legs'. Nothing about *'we've* all got legs'. You could tell by the jaunty cartoon-style of the writing that she was glad about the camper-van conking out, so glad indeed, that I suspected she might have sabotaged it deliberately so that we'd have to seek bodily self-empowerment.

'OK, Greens,' I said. 'Looks like it's befriend our legs time.'

Daniel had had the same idea. 'Come on, girls,' he said. 'This way.'

We set off towards the church tower on the horizon. Daniel was the leader. (As he always was.)

But a slow going we had of it. The horizon kept moving further off. As did the church tower. Elizabeth sank down on a damp grassy tussock to contemplate her stubby little hands. Tilly kept putting up her arms for a carry. The fields were waterlogged.

We walked. We walked. We were like a straggle of refugees. We were the wandering tribes of Israel. We were the dispossessed travelling without hope.

'Let's pretend we're pilgrims!' said Georgie in a courageous attempt to raise morale.

'Which ones?' I asked. 'The Pilgrim Fathers in Massachusetts who discovered turkeys? Or the European ones who crawled along on their knees to find the saint's relic in its holy shrine?'

Before we had time to decide which type of pilgrims we wanted to be, to everybody's surprise, and especially Daniel's who hadn't a clue where we were despite being the leader, we stumbled upon a potato-clamp on the edge of a swampy meadow.

Edwina recognized a familiar landmark. It was the same one they'd nicked the potatoes from. She instantly cheered up.

'Hurrah! Hurray! Hip hip! Isss the goblinsss' cassstle!' she shouted and began to climb up the heap yelling that she was the king of the castle. Tilly scrambled after her. They both slid down the other side. Elizabeth sighed and had another sit-down.

Two fields beyond, already fading into the dusk, I spied the rear of a sprawling dog-eared farm.

I was fed up with Daniel always being the leader. 'You stay here,' I said. 'I'm going over there, to ask the way to the supermarket.'

I strode off on my own, but Georgie came splashing after me. 'Hey, Jewells! Wait for me! I'm not a little one and I'm not staying behind with Daniel.'

I was all for going on down the road. Just as well she came too for it was she who noticed the farm shop. It was at the back of a draughty byre lit by a flickering fluorescent strip.

No shampoo, conditioner, or chocolate. But much else that the greenly spiritual and meditationally artistic parent could desire for the well-being of her children.

We bought carrots (beta carotene), cabbage (chlorophyll, vitamin C), a bag of oats (polyunsaturated fats, B vitamins, calcium, potassium, vitamin E), some swedes, parsnips, turnips, eggs, leeks, and other knobbly brown fruits of the earth that I didn't recognize.

I also bought a few more potatoes. 'Whadyou want them for?' said Georgie. 'We got plenty of spuds at home.'

'These aren't for *us*, stupid,' I hissed under my breath. 'They're to put back on the clamp.'

'Put *back*? What for?' said Georgie so loudly I thought the farmer's wife would hear.

'Because, whatever Daniel says to the contrary, I know stealing is *wrong*.' There are certain things an elder sister has to do. One of them is to impart moral responsibility to her nearest and dearest.

'You're the stupid one. We'll never manage to carry this lot,' Georgie grumbled.

The farmer's wife was packing our stuff into cardboard cartons.

'There you go, my girls,' she said. 'That'll make it easier. Need a hand carrying it out?'

Did she think we'd got a Land Rover waiting for us outside?

'No thanks,' I said. 'We're fine. We're both very strong.' And, in some ways, we probably were.

But not strong enough. Not for Sarsaparilla's type of life. None of us were. Daniel least of all. He was the first to crack.

When Daniel's Heart Was Pierced

You wouldn't believe what a fantastic meal I made that evening. Those oatmeal flapjacks were scrumptious. They all said so (even if adding the chopped onion wasn't such a good idea). And the baked swedes with cheese and parsnip mash weren't bad either.

But being filled fit to bursting wasn't enough to make life sweet.

Day by day, more bad things came about. Tilly got a runny tummy. I won't go into details but you don't have to be an experienced childcarer or even very imaginative to appreciate what it was like having a toddler in an ashram without a washing-machine, and where the mother-figure didn't hold with disposables because they used up too many of the world's treasured resources to fabricate, and would not bio-degrade in less than a hundred thousand years.

Then, Edwina got crusty spots on her face. They made her look a bit unattractive. They were orangey-red.

'At least they match the colour of your hair,' I said, trying to cheer her up. But it made her cry. 'I'm sure they'll go away soon.'

'Not for years, they won't. They're teenage spots. S'pect she's caught them off Daniel,' said Georgie with a knowing grin.

'Don't be silly, Georgie,' I said. 'Whoever heard of a seven year old with acne? I expect it's chilblains.' We'd all had chilblains on our toes.

But Georgie was determined to make Daniel be the cause of Edwina's crusty bits. 'Then it'll be his athlete's foot. Have you seen his feet? They're really horribly fungal. In fact, it's amazing we haven't all caught something off him.'

Edwina's facial splodges weren't helped by her picking at them.

I said to Daniel, 'I just hope it doesn't turn out to be eczema because then we'll have to have that goat. And goats need milking twice a day and I'm not sure I'm up to it.'

'Goat!' said Daniel. 'Who said anything about getting a goat?'

'Sassy did. You remember. Yesterday, when she sent us that long message about the importance of saving the rare breeds of animal from extinction because the multinational corporations were trying to breed them out of existence.'

'We are *not* having a goat!' said Daniel angrily, almost as though he was the parent in charge. 'No way! It's out of the question!'

'Calm down. I expect it was just a passing idea she had.'

'She has too many passing ideas.' He began to work himself up into a fury about her. 'And she gets them all wrong. Quite wrong. One after another. She never thinks her thoughts through. She never sticks with anything.'

'She means well,' I said half-heartedly. I had no idea why I felt I had to stick up for her.

'No she doesn't. All that daft stuff about the Coming of the Cosmic God. Then Pantheism, and ley-lines, and Qui and Li. And if it's not goat-breeding next, it'll be Chinese medicine herbs.'

'You think it's all mumbo-jumbo?'

'No I don't. It only seems that way because she only half knows about it. Like this Shen she's been writing to us about. It wouldn't be so much nonsense if she followed it through but she can't be bothered to study anything properly. She's just a jackdaw, picking up a bit here, a bit there. Next week it'll be crystal dowsing. After that, she'll start stealing our dreams so she can do dream-divining. And before we know where we are she'll be wanting to clear our energy pathways with Feng Shui.'

I laughed. Because there were no cupboards, or wardrobes, we could never put anything away. The pots and pans, plates and spoons were laid about the kitchen floor. Same with our clothes upstairs. Elysian Fields was in such a mess that the only way anybody could clear any kind of pathway through would be if we carried everything outside and put it in the yard.

'Not such a bad idea,' said Daniel. 'Get rid of the lot. *Tabula rasa*. Seriously, Jewells, somehow she's got to be made to concentrate. One thing at a time.'

'But it's not like it's witchcraft or anything wicked.' I was defending our spiritual leader not only because she was the only one we'd got, but also because I knew that it was illegal for children under sixteen to live on their own, however much they may think they want to. 'And it's *not* because she can't be bothered. It's because she's got so much else to do.'

'So much to do?' Daniel guffawed his contempt. 'Like what? *We* do all the work round here. Well, *you* do most of it. The rest of us help a bit.'

Daniel was paying me a compliment. Probably he hadn't meant to. But I was pleased he'd noticed how I did a lot more than my share on the rota.

He said, 'These days, she hardly does *anything* for the family except hand out cash when we ask.'

I said, 'She's preparing for her exhibition.'

'Who does she think she is? Picasso? No decent gallery's ever going to take on her work. They'll see it's all half-baked, just bits and pieces of other artists' ideas.'

I wondered how he knew what was real art and what was non-art. Perhaps Ralph had taught him. Ralph had been a painter too, long ago, when Sarsaparilla was Jane, and Daniel was a baby.

'They don't hold together, do they? One moment she's on crayons trying to be an impressionist. Another day, it's cow-gum and twigs and it might be nursery school. Then it's pebbles in water. There's no overall plan, no consistent vision. She is a complete time-waster.'

'You shouldn't talk about her like that.'

'Even when it's the truth?'

'She's your mother.'

'Yours too.'

'You know what I mean.' I meant, it was much worse when he said what he truly thought about her than when I did.

'That's what worries me. What if it's genetic? What if I end up a mess like her?'

'Don't be stupid! You've got your fifty per cent Ralphness too.'

After that outburst, Daniel kept his negative opinions to himself. Unfortunately, Daniel silent was a whole heap worse than Daniel angry.

Sarsaparilla used to know, or claimed she knew, when any of her chitterlings were distressed.

'It is as if the sharp pain of grief was piercing through the core of my very own heart,' she used to say.

Obviously, being a collectable, I'd never expected her to notice when *I* stomped around feeling as miserable as a wet cat in a thunderstorm. But with blood being supposed to be so thick, she ought to have noticed Daniel. And she ought, surely, to have done something about him?

Any caring mother would. They'd have comforted him in his sadness, talked to him, endeavoured to discover what troubled him. They'd have tried to make their one and only beloved son feel better.

Daniel had always been more of a solitary type than us girls. Now he retreated ever deeper inside the hood of his parka. He spent more time out wooding on his own, and brooding. He dragged his sleeping-bag out of the main bedroom, and across the landing, down three steps and into the poky little space under the stairs. Hardly a room. More of a triangular tent-shape. None of us were meant to know what he did in there once he'd barricaded himself in so tightly that even Tilly couldn't worm her way through. But I guessed. He always took a candle with him and a box of matches, and he still had his books.

Georgie said, 'You mean you think he's still trying to finish his homework? He doesn't usually take so long.'

'Something like that,' I said. 'Trying not to lose all his education.'

If I ever have to have children (O, Lord, defend me from such a fate), I have decided that I shall closely monitor their emotions. If they show the faintest sign of any unhappiness, I shall gather them up into my arms and cuddle them, tickle them, feed them milk chocolate drops, hug them, kiss them, bake them butterfly cakes, buy them buns, sing to them, hum to them, read to them, tell them stories in which they are always the heroes, until they remember how much they are loved and they begin to feel better.

Not Sarsaparilla. She didn't go in for that kind of sentimentality any more. Between rain showers, she pulled her blanket over her shoulders and ventured out to the woods where she found herself some lichen which she carried indoors as respectfully as if it were the consecrated eucharistic host and she nailed it noisily on to a stump of half-rotten wood.

The hammer blows reverberated round Elysian Fields like the doleful sound of iron nails going into a coffin lid.

[This last sentence is not my own work but another of those that I purloined from Daniel's notebooks after he'd gone.]

When My Foster Brother, Daniel Green, Caught the Bus

Deep in sleep, through the dreamy mist of pizzas and chocolates and profiteroles and chocolate profiteroles and peachy ice-cream and peaches and cream and peaches and cream ice-cream I knew that it was my turn on the rota. However good this scrummy dream I Had To Wake Up and Get Up.

Only half awake, I pulled on my boots and duffle coat. It was early, murky, and still half-dark. Mr Churchill in his cage on the windowsill downstairs would be just about getting ready to go to bed.

I went stumbling down to do my family duty.

You had to be ahead of the herd if you were cooking breakfast, otherwise it was like being on a crowded platform during rush-hour at Victoria Station. [This was not my own expression. I got it from Sarsaparilla's old mum. It's what she used to say whenever she came round to tea after school, bringing us those prayer cards and holy pictures and palm crosses that Sarsaparilla didn't approve of.]

I wished we could be back in those days, when Sarsaparilla's mum had been around, instead of in these days.

There was a lot to do, preparing breakfast in an ashram. Select the driest kindling. Find matchbox (cunningly hidden in a different place every day to stop Tilly finding it first). Start fire. Kettle on. Wash out big saucepan (usually caked with burned-on beans from evening before whenever it was my turn on breakfast even though person on evening duty was supposed to have washed it up). As I floundered into the kitchen, scattering mouse droppings and tripping over twigs and muddy boots, I got such a shock it woke me up at once.

Everything ready. Fire glowing. Kettle steaming. Big blue tea-pot with cracked spout and no lid brewing (four tea-bags). Porridge bubbling.

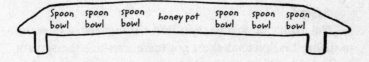

were set neatly on table. Enough dry wood was stacked up as if to last for ever.

woodwoodwoodwoodwood
woodwoodwoodwoodwoodwood
woodwoodwoodwoodwoodwoodwood
woodwoodwoodwoodwoodwoodwoodwood
woodlogwoodlogwoodlogwoodlogwoodlogwoodlog

Daniel was by the windowsill cleaning out Mr Churchill's cage. His rucksack (Daniel's, not Mr Churchill's) was on the floor by the door like a crouching dog straining to leap. He (Daniel again, not Mr Churchill) grunted a sort of good morning.

I said, 'What's up?'

'Off today,' he said.

I said, 'What?'

'Going.'

'You're going?'

'Yep.'

'Well, I can see that. Where?'

'Where d'you think?'

'How should I know?'

This rally, with him bluffing and me asking, went on for a couple more rounds till he said, 'Ralph's place.'

'Back to your *dad*? To *live*?' I gasped.

He didn't reply, just stood there looking at the floor. So, after a bit, I said in a more normal voice, 'I thought you couldn't trust him?'

He shrugged. 'Yup. On and off. But it'll just be for a while. Not for ever. See how it goes.'

I gulped. I said, 'It's a big thing to do.'

He said, 'It's *her* I can't stand.'

'Sassy?'

'No, Lulu. Ralph's woman. But I'll manage. I'm going to ignore her, pretend she's not there, or she's the servant or something.'

'I wish you hadn't got to go.'

'I'll come back and see you now and then.'

I didn't believe he would. But it was nice of him to say it.

I got Sarsaparilla's breakfast tray ready, with the positive-energy honey not the negative sugar. I said, 'You take it up. Then you can tell her.'

'No. You tell her. After I've gone.'

What a wimp. And how was Sarsaparilla going to

react? What if she had some kind of fit up there in her artist's eyrie, because of her high-blood-pressure thing? What if she pined to death for her brown-eyed boy?

But when the rest of them came galumphing down like a herd of buffaloes there was no time to worry whether my brother was a coward. He was at least prepared to tell his sisters, if not his mother, that he was leaving.

'Hooray, hooray!' cried Tilly clapping her hands in her porridge. She cheered any family announcement. How was she to know the difference between the good and the bad?

Elizabeth joined in any clapping or cheering. 'Hip hip hippo!' she grinned.

Georgie didn't cheer. 'It's really stupid of you,' she said. 'Stupid, stupid. It's *brilliant* here. Apart from the food.'

Daniel said, 'I've got used to the dirt and the food. It's not the being here I mind. It's the not going to school.'

'School!' Georgie shrieked. 'You *hated* school!' Was she so angry because she was upset about him going? Or because she hadn't truly got used to the dirt and the cold?

'Maybe I hated *that* school. But I never bunked off all the time like Jewells, did I? I knew I'd got to go every day. I don't want to be an ignorant moron. I want to be educated. It's the only way out. I can't live in a muddle. Nobody can.'

'We *don't* live in a muddle!' said Georgie fiercely. 'Look over there. I tidied up all that stuff on the floor yesterday.' She'd stacked the plates and bowls in a neat pile in the corner so we wouldn't keep standing on them by mistake. '*And* I've made Elizabeth's bed.'

'I mean mental muddle. I want to study, learn new things, take exams, pass them and get to college. I want to be able to do a proper job when I grow up. I want a *normal* kind of life.'

'What's wrong with this life?' snarled Georgie. 'Too good for you, is it?'

I knew what Daniel wanted even if Georgie was pretending she didn't. I, too, had this private yearning to sit in a warm corner of a quiet library and read a story book I'd never read before.

'You always think you're so super-strong and clever, don't you,' Georgie went on ranting. 'So I suppose you're going to *fly* back to your dad's wonderful place then? Or are you going to walk?'

I said, 'No wonder he wants to leave if you keep on needling him.'

Daniel stayed calm. 'Ralph would've fetched me if I'd asked. But you know it's better if he doesn't come here.'

'Ashamed of us, are you?'

'Of course not.'

'So you're taking a taxi, are you?' Georgie snarled.

'Bus, actually.'

'Bus!' Georgie shrieked. 'That's a joke. When did anybody last see a *bus* round here?'

'I'll make some sandwiches for your journey,' I said quietly.

Daniel said, 'There's a stop opposite the farm shop.'

Georgie said, 'Well *I've* never seen it.'

Nor had I. But if Daniel was determined, he'd have checked it out. It occurred to me later (being a slow thinker) that the reason Georgie was angry was because deep down she wanted to get away too. But she couldn't because she hadn't got a known dad to escape to and her blood mother wasn't allowed to have her because of being too fervent in her faith.

'We'll go with him,' I said, pushing Edwina's jacket and scarf at her. 'Just as far as the farm shop.' I had an idea I could ask the farm shop woman about the facial splodges which weren't getting any better despite the Chinese herbs.

'No way,' said Edwina folding her arms across her front so I couldn't force her arms down the sleeves. She was right to resist. Who'd want to go out on a cold walk in the drizzle?

'We'll get something extra delicious. A treat,' I said, to bribe her.

'Sssomssing really nissse?'

'Of course,' I said, wondering what it would be. A sackful of root vegetables?

'Not just ssswedesss?' said Edwina.

'No, something *really* nice.'

We left Georgie grumpily minding Elizabeth and Tilly. Daniel set a fast pace. Edwina was soon trailing far behind. Daniel had to wait for her to catch up and give her a piggy-back.

When we reached the farm shop, there, tucked into the hedge, just as Daniel had said it would be, was a bus stop. No shelter, no bench, just a scratched metal post with a plasticized timetable attached.

It would seem that, in life, people only see what they're looking for. Daniel had been looking for a bus stop. I didn't yet know what I was looking for, apart from a convincing bribe for Edwina or she'd never trust me again.

We had to wait two hours. This was only an estimate. None of us owned a watch any more. It felt more like three hours. But I knew from experience that when you're waiting for something, be it a bus or a kettle or a birthday, time goes more slowly. So I knocked off a third of the estimated time of waiting. Eventually, the bus came lumbering along the lane.

Daniel was the only passenger. He wouldn't kiss either of us goodbye, let alone hug us, but he muttered, 'See you then,' and he gave us each a sharp thump on the upper arm. A curious demonstration of fraternal affection. But better than none.

'Good riddance,' I said which was the nearest I could get to returning affection.

Daniel bought his ticket from the driver, then leaned out and handed me all the loose cash from his pocket. 'Spend wisely,' he said as the doors swished shut.

We watched the bus disappear between the hedges with Daniel's hand still waving like a white feather at the rear window.

'Ssso whasss thisss nissse sssurprissse you gonna get me?' Edwina asked.

What indeed?

I crossed over to the farm shop. She followed closely like a duckling. The farmer's wife in her checked apron was there, same as usual. The rough, sand-encrusted carrots, potatoes, swedes, and parsnips were heaped in their wooden bins, same as usual. The coarse green cabbages were sprawling in a broken barrow, same as usual. The mucky free-range eggs were in their tray on the wooden counter.

There was something else as well and suddenly I knew that Sarsaparilla's mum was right. Miracles could happen.

Alongside the dirty eggs sat a row of cakes, every one different. There had never been cakes before.

The farmer's wife saw me staring. 'All home baked,' she said. 'Just this morning.'

Edwina gaped at the fruit cake, the apricot slice cake, the iced cherry lattice cake, the jam sponge, then stared at me as though I'd made the miracle myself.

'You choose,' I said airily. 'While I get the other stuff.'

She spent so long dithering between cherry lattice and lemon drizzle sponge that by the time I remembered to ask about her facial splodges, we were halfway home. And Edwina talked and fretted about the cake all the way.

'What'sss Sssasssy gonna sssay? We ssshould eat it quick, you and me, ssso ssshe won't sssee. It'sss sssugar, isssn't it? It'sss negative energy. Ssshe'll be ssso crosss wisss usss.'

'Course we can't eat it now. That wouldn't be fair. It's for all of us.' It wasn't a very large lemon drizzle cake. In fact, it was just the right size for two hungry girls transporting a load of vegetables in rucksacks. However, I knew the importance of imparting a code of good moral conduct to those younger than oneself.

'To consume the cake secretly would be deceitful,' I said. 'Not sharing it would be greedy.'

Certain things in life, however, were never for sharing. I'd always wanted a room of my own. Always, for as long as I'd been alive. That night, I moved out of the girls' room and into the tent-shaped space under the stairs. The ceiling sloped so sharply that you could only stand upright in the doorway. Daniel's sleeping-bag was still spread out on the floor and most of his books were still there too, arranged round the wainscoting like a draught-excluder. *Teach Yourself Physics, How to Become a Top-dog Mathematician, French Grammar part II, Les Histoires de Rosalie* (foreign), *Geology for Fun, Science for Beginners.* Pity he wasn't more interested in story books.

On one side, a round window, no bigger than a plate, looked directly out into the bare branches of the trees. I remembered how Sarsaparilla said we only had to make friends with the trees and they'd talk to us and give us our education.

I thought I'd give Daniel's books a try first.

How Some Sunny Days Came Back Again

The morning after Daniel's departure, the weather turned.

My little space under the stairs was filled with golden sunbeams. And I could hear Edwina singing outside in the yard even before Georgie had measured out the porridge oats. I saw her through the little round window, prancing around the yard in her nightie. There was no point in yelling at her that she'd got to come in and put on more clothes else she'd catch her death of cold because it was obviously so much warmer out there than it was inside.

I went out to join her in the beautiful brightness.

'Sssmagic!' she sang. 'Ssswe been magicked!'

'Have we?' I said and I found the air was soft and sweet to breathe.

'I sssaid, ssslike we'sss been sss'magicked to another country. Sss'Africa. S'ssnot like it usssed to be. S'ss all different. Sss'fantassstic!'

The sky overhead was as blue and clear as Elizabeth's tiny periwinkle eyes while the new grass was as green as Edwina's. The sun shone so warm that it was steaming the water out of the puddles, the dew off the bushes, the mould out of our washing on the line.

Georgie brought the porridge and honey out to us. We sat on logs. Insects shimmered in the air like fairies. Birds chirruped from the trees. We listened to the shiny crackle of crocus petals opening to the sun. We put our ears to the ground to catch the sound of the grass growing and the moles waking up.

'Bad luck for poor old Daniel,' said Georgie. 'Missing out on this. Isn't it a *shame*?' I could tell by the smirk in her smile that she felt he deserved to miss any good moments we might have as punishment for his defection. I knew that the sudden climate change had nothing to do with his leaving. Nonetheless, a reflective person such as I was couldn't help *wondering* if it was Daniel's antagonistic state of mind which had been holding spring at bay.

'Let's pretend we're in one of those hot countries,' said Georgie.

'We don't have to pretend,' I said.

Georgie pulled off her jersey. She had three more jerseys under it. 'Let's do that sun-bathing thing then, shall we?' she said. She took off two more jerseys.

'Good idea,' I said.

I dragged a blanket on to the grass for Elizabeth to lie on. I rolled down my chalet leg-warmers (formerly known as chalet-socks, but now footless and unravelling) and exposed my bare bluish legs. Tilly pulled off her own nappy.

We lounged around, relaxing peacefully. Tilly found a long piece of binder-twine on the ground. She toddled about trailing it behind her pretending she had a dog on a lead. The only disturbance to an otherwise perfect morning was when she waddled too far, got caught in brambles and started barking for help and had to be rescued. There was another disturbance when Edwina asked if anybody knew how to make a daisy-chain.

'Haven't a clue,' said Georgie, remaining motionlessly flat on her back with her eyes closed.

I didn't feel like sitting up either. I said, 'Not now, Edwina. We're relaxing. I'll show you another day.'

'Sssere won't be any flowersss nexsst time,' Edwina whined and I was about to relent and show her when I saw that we had a visitor, our first visitor.

He was walking up our track. He'd left his van parked in the lane. He was leading Tilly by the hand. She'd wandered off again with her imaginary dog without us noticing. We all stared at the van, then at the man as he puffed towards us with Tilly waddling beside him. She was beaming as though she'd found a new toy, better than any invisible dog. I felt a frightening tightening in my stomach. What if this was her blood father come to fetch her away? Sarsaparilla would be in despair to lose two of her chicks in less than a day. But he was too old. He had white hair, more like somebody's grandad.

Georgie said, 'Suppose she's being *kidnapped*?'

I said sharply, 'If he's a kidnapper, he'd hardly be bringing her *back* to us, would he?'

I was normally a well-mannered person and I liked to impart my good manners to my sisters. So, staring like wombats, was, I now realize, a rude reception to offer any visitor. (I realize a lot of things about the past since I got more mature. And I'm a lot more mature than I used to be. Everybody says so.)

Georgie got up from the grass. 'And how may I help you?' she said in a hoity-toity voice like she was the princess of the castle. Just because she'd done the porridge she thought she was the boss, not that she'd cleared up like she was supposed to.

'I'm your leccy, dear,' said the old man. He held out the identification card on a chain round his neck but Georgie wasn't a great one for reading small print, or large.

'You what?' she said.

'Come to check your system and read the meter.'

'We don't need reading,' I said.

'Is your mum home? Or your dad?'

'She's upstairs,' said Georgie.

'She's busy,' I said. 'She's working.'

'No ssshe'sss not,' said Edwina. 'Ssshe'sss lying on Missster Sssingh'sss bedsssspreadsss sssstaring at the ssseiling asss missserable as sssin.'

I remembered one should never admit to being part of a single-parent family or people took advantage of you. I said, 'Well anyway, our parents are unavailable and cannot currently be disturbed so if there is something requires a signature, I have full authority to sign on behalf.'

With a flush of freedom, I realized that certain things were already a lot better without Daniel. Without him cluttering up the place, I could exercise more of my Own Personal Authority (provided Georgie didn't elbow her way in ahead of me).

To demonstrate my OPA I followed the visitor indoors and watched him like a fox as he did whatever he was supposed to do, which seemed to involve poking around in dark corners with a torch and unscrewing our light switches.

'Hm. Dicey,' he said.

'What dicey?'

'Wiring you got here. None too safe.'

'We know. That's why we don't use the switches more than we can help. They quite often crackle when you touch them.'

'Whole caboodle needs re-wiring,' he said, tapping information into an electronic note-pad. 'As a matter of urgency.'

'Yes,' I said. 'We were just about to have it done.'

'So they got rid of the squatters?'

'What squatters?'

'Not to worry, dear. I'll drop a word to the housing people at the council. They ought to get a move on. Provide more amenities. It's medieval out here, isn't it? If you don't keep prodding, they ignore you half the time, don't they? No street lighting. No post office. No phone box. But we all pay our taxes. We all got rights. There'll be a grant towards the re-wiring if I'm not mistaken.'

'Actually, we don't live here. We're here on holiday,' I suddenly said.

I could tell he didn't believe me.

'Sort of adventure camping.' Why did I lie to a stranger? Was I ashamed of the way we lived, with our dirty dishes piling up round the sink, mouse droppings all over the table and artworks hanging from the banisters as though the trees had walked indoors? Did I want to pretend our chaos was only temporary and that we actually enjoyed it?

'Can't leave it like this,' he said.

'It's all right, I was just going to do it,' I said because I thought he meant the burned-on porridge pan that Georgie had left on the floor.

He didn't. He was still on about electricity. 'I'm going to have to cut you off. Be more than my job's worth to leave it.'

'Doesn't matter,' I said airily. 'That's what this type of adventure scheme's about. We've been learning to be back-to-nature and self-reliant.' I was about to explain that we were doing our Duke of Edinburgh Bronze awards. But then I caught sight of Edwina and Tilly outside, both trailing bits of string as though they had dogs and I realized that more lies wouldn't necessarily make me sound more convincing.

He gave me a printed leaflet. It explained how to get the power restored. 'Give it to your parents, won't you now?'

'Of course. As soon as they've finished their work,' I said. Such a responsible child.

He'd driven off in his van before the artistic recluse descended. She was tousled and slightly sad, though not all puffy so she can't have been howling her heart out unless her tears were the invisible kind. She was surprisingly composed about Daniel leaving.

'A wise mother knows she can't hold on to her children for ever. You have to relinquish them when they're ready, for the wind always bloweth where it listeth.'

I nodded and tried to look encouraging. It must have worked because she enfolded me in a bone-cracking hug.

'Ah, my sweetie-moppet. Praise the Lord that I still have you.'

I showed her the leaflet about the electricity. But she didn't seem to be in the right mood for leaflet-reading.

'Not now, petkins. You see, Daniel has unwittingly revealed an important truth to me. About communication.'

'I think this may be an important truth too,' I said, flapping the leaflet in front of her face.

'Concerning communication. Face to face. Heart to heart. Word to word. Lip to lip. Communication by word of mouth is the only truth we have. So, my love, there will be no more notes between us. That is a promise.'

'Rightio. If you say so,' I said. She'd made many promises in my lifetime.

'You know what, flowerpot?' She enfolded me in another embrace. 'It's been so deathly quiet all morning, I wondered what on *earth* was going on. I'd begun to think you'd *all* left home!'

'Course not. Daniel may blow where he listeth but I don't. Look, I'm making a picnic to take outside.'

I piled cold cooked potatoes, cold leftover parsnip mash, and a brick of bread into a basket. I added a bottle of sandy tap-water.

'Oh, I see. You've been playing outside today, have you?'

Play? When did I last have time to play? A short spell of sun-bathing. That was all. Mostly it was work, work, work.

I said, 'You should come out with us too. Do you good. Get some sun on your skin. Make your own vitamin D.'

'A *picnic*? What a *clever* idea!' she said as though it was something quite novel.

'Yes. To get outside and meet people. You've been on your own too long.'

Showing considerable OPA, I led the way. Sarsaparilla followed obediently, blinked in the bright sun, then lowered herself onto the blanket and settled down beside Elizabeth, her big white legs and chunky arms exposed to the sunrays.

'Ooh là là!, my darlings! This is just like the south of France. When I was a student—did I ever tell you, popkins?—I was there, on a painting course. A simply gorgeous little place. Near where that sad man cut off his ear. So passionate! The sky was just this same colour. And I remember the sun! So hot Ralph had to buy me a hat.'

It would probably have been all right if Edwina hadn't mentioned how we'd had a visitor. Sarsaparilla stopped reminiscing and became upset.

'Snooping, was he, your visitor?'

'No,' I said. 'He came to read the meter. Only he couldn't find it. So he had to search around a bit.'

'Lambkin, you should not let strangers in, you know that, however kind they may seem. Don't do it again, will you?'

'He was only doing his job,' I said. And so was I.

'But, sweetie, now we can't even have the lights on.'

I didn't like being told off when I hadn't done anything wrong (except, of course, for telling a lie to the electrician about being on holiday, but Sarsaparilla didn't know that). 'As a matter of fact, if you must know,' I said in a huff, 'it wasn't just the wiring he was on about. He didn't like the look of the fireplace either. He said we ought to have a guard round it.'

'I dare say he's right, poppet,' said Sarsaparilla, patting me on the head as though I was Tilly's new dog. 'We should. First thing tomorrow. Remind me to see to it.'

I should have told her there and then to do something about it, snip-snap-quick, because we were all at risk. But I forgot. Or perhaps I couldn't be bothered. And anyway, why was it always up to *me* to take responsibility for the domestic arrangements? I always knew she was a lousy inattentive mother.

Fire! Fire!
Fetch the Engines

Cold grey potatoes, cold beige parsnips, hard dark bread aren't nearly as bad as you expect they're going to be, providing you're eating them out of doors on a bright day in spring. Even the water tasted less gritty than usual. Sarsaparilla said it was as delicious as elderflower champagne.

'That's what we must do later on,' she decided. 'As soon as the elderflowers are in bloom, we will come out and gather bushels of blooms to ferment our own elderflower wine!'

'Great idea, Sassy,' I said in what I hoped was a convincing tone because there was no point in spoiling a lovely day by pointing out that she was the only person old enough to be legally allowed to drink any wine that we might succeed in making.

The kittens were as affected by the change of season

as the rest of us. They joined us on the grass, nuzzling against our feet, then sniffing through our picnic. When they realized we had nothing that they liked eating, they gambolled off through the brackens and ferns, deeper into the wood.

Edwina's dog wandered after them. Then Tilly's did too. So then Edwina and Tilly both went charging off after their two invisible hounds. Next thing, the rest of us were joining in and it had turned into a tiger-hunt. We went further and further. Georgie and I imagined we were intrepid explorers finding our way through the Amazonian rainforest. Sarsaparilla had to take my arm for support over fallen logs and crocodiles. Georgie helped Elizabeth keep the leeches off her legs.

Dappled sunlight flickered down through the bare branches like stardust. The bark of the tree-trunks glowed with a silvery sheen. We watched squirrels slithering and scrambling and leaping along the upper branches like tropical monkeys. We heard hollow hammering.

'Hearken to the distant beat of the jungle drums,' I said. 'Speaking from village to village across the vast Saharan wastes.'

Georgie said, 'I thought this was the Amazon?'

'Same difference,' I said.

'OK,' said Georgie agreeably.

'Girls, did you hear that? The lesser spotted woodpecker, if I'm not mistaken,' said Sarsaparilla. Our stately African queen may have thought it was a woodpecker. Georgie and I knew it was jungle drums.

In a wide clearing, we came upon a sweep of small white flowers nodding in the breeze.

'Orchids!' I said. 'The rarest in the world.'

Sarsaparilla, who remained unaware that we were in a sweltering central African rainforest, said, 'Aah, wind anemones. Sweetest of all the harbingers of spring.'

The strangely idyllic afternoon put our ambulant artist into an increasingly poetic mood. She threw back her head and started to yodel. 'See how we skip upon the trees of paradise, paradise, paradise!'

'Whassat?' said Edwina.

'It's meant to be some kind of special mountain singing,' I said. 'It means she's happy.'

But she was too happy. We all were. It is always dangerous to be happy. You never know what'll be lurking round the next corner, ready to scare you.

If only we hadn't gone out like that, believing we were in heaven, or Africa or South America. If only one of us had had the foresight to stay behind then they'd have been there to smell the smoke, to spot the spark, to raise the alarm before it was too late. The only member of the family we'd left behind was Mr Churchill, asleep under his home-made duvet of chewed-up newspaper, snug in the sleeping compartment of his cage, upon the kitchen windowsill beside the door.

Sarsaparilla was still warbling as we ambled home, admiring the equinoctial sun going down in its golden blaze of glory. Already, Elysian Fields was on its way towards eternal destruction. We all noticed the smoke puffing busily from the closed windows, from the cracks in the bricks, seeping outwards through the messy thatch.

We got closer to the house. Some of us began to run towards it. We heard a sharp pinging. We didn't know it then but it was the sound of window panes cracking, of baked bean tins swelling and exploding.

We began to rush this way and that, like hungry hamsters searching for fresh grains. Except we were looking for buckets, cans, plastic cups, bottles, broken cups, anything that would hold water. Where was water?

The element that had been pouring so persistently down from the heavens when we didn't want it, was now in short supply. The tiny brass tap was over the sink in the smoke-filled kitchen. We couldn't reach it.

'Go to the water butt!' yelled Georgie, quick-thinking. We ran across the yard with our cups, jugs, and leaky buckets. We lowered them right down to the bottom of the butt for it was practically empty.

'Sassy's been using it,' I said. All those earthy water-washes wasting a precious element.

Our splashes and sprinkles dampened the outer walls but the smoke was increasing into a fog so thick we could scarcely see each other.

Sarsaparilla let out a cry of pain. 'Aaagheeeh!' I thought she must have dropped a bucket on her foot. She rushed towards the kitchen door. 'The homage to the courage of Mother Nature!' she wailed. 'The best work of my entire life!' She pushed open the door and blundered in.

Being such a very substantial person, when she moved she displaced a lot of air. Moving air is the favourite food of fire. Sarsaparilla's rushing was providing a feast. (The moral, if you happen to be a very large person in a potential fire situation, is: stand very still or you'll only make things worse.)

The moment that Sarsaparilla rushed into the smoking house, the golden sparks began to leap out through the thatch like glow-worms in the dusk.

Tilly clapped her hands. 'Oooooh!' she cooed.

It was sensational, as if the whole roof was covered in birthday sparklers. Then I remembered that it wasn't only Sarsaparilla and the Mother Nature artworks who were in there. There was also the smallest and least-demanding member of the family, the widower, for whom night was day and day was night. He'd be snuffling quietly in his bed. And even if he was woken by the smoke, there was nothing he could do from behind his bars except bear witness to the tragedy unfolding before his bright brown eyes.

'Mr Churchill!' I gasped. I started to follow Sarsaparilla but didn't even reach the front door before I was caught and trapped by the yellow and black of steely strong arms. There were firefighters all over the place and more running up the track.

Then the big flames started.

Then There Were Seven (If You Counted Mr Churchill)

They went shooting into the sky like scarlet rockets.

Three fire engines were already in the lane. One was stuck in the mud. The other two ground their way up the track. I hadn't even heard the sirens.

A week later, Richard explained to me that when people are going through a traumatic event their senses are distorted so they may hear or feel things differently. I realized that I am obviously one of those ultra-sensitive people for whom all feelings are flattened out by the shock of a crisis.

However, I knew that my smarting, streaming eyes were not deceiving me when I saw Sarsaparilla emerge from Elysian Fields. She had streaming, bloodshot eyes, a runny nose, and an old man's raspy voice.

'Smoke. Too much. Too hot. Stairs gone. Couldn't find stairs. Couldn't find life's work. All gone. Everything.'

But not everybody had gone. In her grimy hands she clutched Mr Churchill's cage.

'How many?' one of the firefighters asked.

'Just one,' I said. 'His life's companion died a while back. He's been on his own ever since.'

But it wasn't the quantity of hamsters trapped in the blaze they were interested in. It was trapped humans.

Sarsaparilla was given some oxygen out of a cylinder to breathe so she'd stop panicking. And once she'd calmed down she got a big telling-off from the captain of the brigade. I heard him explaining why you should never enter a burning building, not even to rescue someone sleeping. You could be crushed by falling timber, suffocated by smoke inhalation, electrocuted by live wires. He was going on and on at Sarsaparilla about all the terrible things that might have happened to her. I noticed, despite the traumatic state I was in, that he left out being drowned by the water from their powerful hoses.

'And never ever go back to rescue a pet,' he finished. 'Animals have their own ways of escaping danger.'

Escaping from a closed metal cage? Who was he kidding?

'Mr Churchill is part of our family,' I said. 'No more nor less valued than any other.' I was pleased with that phrase and I hoped that some day some person would use it about me. I'd heard Sarsaparilla use it about Elizabeth when a snotty neighbour said she didn't think that mongy people like that had any purpose to their lives.

I didn't like the way the expert firefighter had been going on at Sarsaparilla as though she'd done something truly wicked. He was making her cry. Not only smoke tears. Real crying. I'd rarely seen Sarsaparilla cry. It was bad to do that to her. Trying to save a hamster and your rustic artworks wasn't a sin. Just misguided. I went and gave her a hug.

'Everything's all right, Sassy,' I said. 'Nobody's hurt. Nobody's missing.'

'And Daniel?' she said.

'He went yesterday, you remember. He wasn't even here when the fire started.'

Shock was making her confused. 'Of course. How silly of me. He left us.'

'And the rest of us are OK, even Mr Churchill's fine. He slept right through.'

An ambulance came doo-dahing up the lane. But there were no serious casualties; at least, not that day. I did a head-count to make sure. We were all there, except for the tiger-kittens who were so terrified by the firemen's water hoses and big wet boots that they raced back into the woods.

None of us knew what caused the fire though there were, in my opinion, four possible explanations, each highly plausible.

'Four? So what are they?' Georgie asked.

'One. Lack of fireguard because Sarsaparilla failed in her duty to get one. A tiny spark jumped out of the hearth and into the kindling pile where it glowed all afternoon until the glow became a flicker and the flicker grew to flame.'

Georgie didn't think much of this theory. 'The fire in the grate wasn't lit,' she said.

'You sure?' I said. 'It was *always* lit, first thing in the morning.'

'I should know. It was me that was on the rota this morning. I let it go out. On purpose as soon as I'd done the porridge.'

'Why on earth did you do that?'

'I was trying to save wood, wasn't I. I thought if we

didn't have Daniel around any more, it was going to be a lot more hard work getting enough wood in.'

'OK. Two. It was Tilly. You know how much she liked playing with the matchbox. Shaking it to make it rattle. The match-heads are phosphorous which can catch itself alight in contact with air. Doesn't sound very likely but it's what Daniel told us and he was usually right.'

Georgie said, 'There weren't any matches in the box. I took them out and gave Tilly the empty box to play with.'

'She might have found the matches.'

'No. I put them in a jam jar up on the mantelpiece.'

'She might have got them when you weren't watching.' I didn't like the way Georgie thought she knew everything. *I* was supposed to be the eldest, the one with the OPA.

'She can't have. She was with us. Every second of every minute. I didn't want her wandering off again. *I* should know. *I* was carrying her most of the time. And her invisible dog. It kept scratching me.'

'How could it? It wasn't a real dog.'

'Yes it was. To Tilly it was. Why d'you always have to be so boringly realistic?'

The shock and upheaval of the fire had made us irritable. Friction by fire.

'So?' I said crossly. 'And suppose it was arson? You gonna rubbish that too?'

But Georgie didn't even know what arson was.

'A deliberate act,' I said.

Georgie said, 'Who'd want to do that?'

'Someone with strange creative ideas about purity and starting life afresh in the Garden of Eden.'

'You mean Sarsaparilla?' said Georgie.

I nodded.

'I don't believe it. She'd never do something like that.'

'Not even if she wanted a *tabula rasa*?' I knew Georgie didn't know what that meant and I was glad. I could exert my superior knowledge and senior position. I said, 'Sassy is a person of extreme artistic temperament. It is entirely possible that she might have deliberately set light to her studio in order to wipe clean the slate and start her creative process anew.'

'I don't believe you,' said Georgie.

I said, '*I* don't want to believe it either. But you have to turn every stone over and look at its other side. *You* didn't see her when she first came downstairs. She was in a highly volatile state, even maybe a bit bonkers.'

'She loves us. She wouldn't want to destroy us.'

'It wasn't *us* she wanted to destroy. It was art.'

Georgie was reluctant to accept my arson theory, if only because it was so scary. 'How *could* she have? We were all together all afternoon picking those flipping wood anemone flowers she kept going on about.'

'No we weren't. Don't you remember? Just when we'd got to the big clearing under the beeches, we lost sight of her.'

'Only for about two minutes. She was sitting on a tree-stump.'

I remembered. And the sight of the wood anemones, spreading like sheets of snow whichever way you looked.

I had only one more idea, one person left to accuse. For some reason I was beginning to assume that it had to be a person who'd done it.

'Daniel.'

'Daniel!' said Georgie. 'How could it be? He'd already gone.'

'But just think about it for a second. He might've come back.'

'Why?'

'To see how we are. Because he missed us. To make sure we were OK.'

Georgie rolled her eyes. 'Yeah. As if.'

'And then he found you'd let the fire go out,' I went on, believing it the more I imagined it happening. 'So he got it going again. He was trying to be helpful to make up for leaving us in the lurch. Then he waited for us to come back and when we didn't he heaped up the wood so the fire'd last and put on too much wood.'

Georgie sighed. 'Yeah yeah. And I've another theory which is just about as cracked. Daniel came zooming back on Ralph's Harley Davidson and poured petrol all over the kitchen floor. Just for spite.'

'Don't be daft. Ralph does *not* have a motorbike.' Ralph was a not very successful graphic artist. He'd once done an ad that was on telly. But it was a long time ago.

'All right. Not a motorbike. They both came back on the bus. And Daniel torched the whole place because he hates us so much.'

'Hates us? Now you're being silly.'

'No sillier than you.'

'Course he didn't hate us. Well, only sometimes he got in a mood with someone. Mostly, he was just fed up being part of a lot of girls. But not enough to want to burn us up like witches.'

That night something far more important than a spontaneous house-fire happened. Georgie's first period started. So I had to be extra nice to her. It wasn't fair. It should have been me first. She's loads younger than me.

How God Moved Mysteriously

The firefighters were obliged to investigate. They were thorough and impartial. It was going to take them a long time to reach a conclusion. They didn't seem interested in my views, even though I knew a lot more about my family and the intricacies of the late departed building than they ever would.

Meanwhile, the farmer, who'd called them on his mobile from his tractor cab when he'd been harrowing a field because he thought the smoke he could see was coming from one of his own strawstacks, had his own theory. It was different from any of mine.

'Lot of damage done by rodents. Specially round this quarter,' he said. 'Chew anything them do. Fully-grown male rat, he'll cut your cables in a twinkle of the eye. Watched them at it I have. Clean through the outer insulations, don't they? Expose your conducting wire, electrocute themselves. Dead before they even know it. Create your short circuit. And bingo, you've a blaze on your hands.' He nodded confidently, fingered his mobile, then added, 'Course, not to omit it's a tragedy you've lost your home, Mrs Green. We all agree on that.'

Sarsaparilla poked with the toe-cap of her boot at a heap of burned fabric on the ground. You could just make out that it had once been one of her favourite swirly curtain-frocks. Now it was crumbling into black wet nothing.

A very long time ago, at least a year back, when I was emotionally a lot younger than I am now, I used to think Sarsaparilla was the worst person in the whole world to have as a parent. I remember telling Daniel how I wouldn't wish her on anybody, not even my worst enemy. I think I might have mentioned this view to Mrs Jeans too. And probably Ralph, and perhaps even Elizabeth, though definitely not Edwina.

I shouldn't have said it to anyone. It was silly and juvenile. I know better now. She might have been unusual, sometimes eccentric, and always unreliable. But, at that time and in those circumstances, standing in a damp meadow in contemplation of the burned-out farmhouse with nothing left, not even a three-legged chair, she seemed like the best mother any of us could have had. I trusted her to hold us together, to help us pull through.

She said, with a distant dreamy smile as though looking for angels, 'Doth not the Almighty move through the cosmos in many mysterious ways? And is there not a season for all things if we had only the eyes to see, yet ours not to reason why?'

It sounded good, even if I didn't understand what it meant.

'So let us rejoice that there is nothing so thoroughly cleansing for the soul than the destruction of earthly possessions,' she went on and I could tell from the way her eyes were upcast to the darkening sky that she was not so much depressed by the situation as exhilarated by the new challenge. 'To be rid of all that weighed us down is like sloughing off the skin of our old lives so that we might start afresh.'

'Whasssat? Whasss ssshe on about now?' said Edwina.

I said, 'How the flip d'you think *I* should know? I'm not your interpreter.'

If I'd known that Edwina was shortly to be removed, pale-faced and stuttering with an explosion of esses, from the bosom of the family and placed in an alien household, I might've chosen to speak more gently to her because I'm not a cruel person. But I didn't know. Back then, though I knew quite a lot, I didn't know everything.

Even before the ambulance (which wasn't required) had finished reversing its way out of the mud in the lane, two more people turned up in a sports car, wanting to find out what was going on. They were a journalist and a photographer. They'd heard the sirens and followed the third fire engine. After living in isolation, it was peculiar to see so many strangers standing around in the meadow and tramping across the yard.

The journalist held a palm-sized sound recorder up to our mouths. 'So how d'you *feel?*' she asked. None of us were too sure. We knew only that we were supposed to be rejoicing that we'd sloughed off our dead skins.

For once, Elizabeth was the only one of us to give a normal reaction to the calamitous conflagration. She was shivering and had to be wrapped in a silver recovery blanket. 'Bad thing, bad thing. Fire,' she said which was, for her, a long statement to make, if not the most scintillating soundbite for the press.

The journalist persisted. Georgie, after much thought, said, 'Actually, I feel a bit hungry.'

Edwina agreed, 'Sssame here. Sssausagessss isss what I feelsss like. Sssvegetarian sssausssagesss wissss ketsssup.' This was quite an original post-incandescence sensation, but since the journalist couldn't understand a word of it, that wasn't much use to her either.

It was Tilly who said the words that caught the journalist's creative imagination. 'Look, look, look, look,' she said. 'Hurrah, hurrah. Sassy. She got him. He hungry girl.' She pushed some withered daisy-heads through the bars of Mr Churchill's cage, then changed her mind, pulled them out and popped them into her mouth.

I learned something important that day which is that if there is one thing which makes a better news story than a family made homeless by fire, it is a small furry creature saved from a fire. The journalist became momentarily enlivened. She asked about Mr Churchill. But, as I explained to her, apart from losing his wife, he had led an eventless life. I told her instead how he'd been named after a great British prime minister who had the same tendency as our Mr Churchill to sleep during the day. But the journalist obviously didn't see there'd be any public interest in this curious fact for she rudely switched off her voice recorder in the middle of me talking and muttered to the photographer, 'Maybe we'd better push the human courage factor. OK?'

But Sarsaparilla hadn't time to give interviews. She was too busy being harassed by some more on-lookers who'd just turned up. They were from social services.

The separation of Sarsaparilla from three of her precious chickadees was executed so swiftly and professionally that the two of us who were not removed from our foster-mother's care hardly even had time to notice it was occurring.

How Sycamores Fly

Georgie and I were the two who were left behind. It was strange to feel so unwanted.

'Growing children,' Sarsaparilla's mum used to tell us, 'are like sycamore seeds. They've got wings to help them fly away when the time is right.'

She'd shown us a seed-pod with its pair of papery propellers. They twirl it far from the tree to a space where it can flourish without competition from other twirling pods.

'We've got wings?' we said, incredulous.

'Of course,' our sort-of nan said. 'But yours are angel wings. So they're invisible.'

Georgie's and my wings were so invisible as to be ineffective. We didn't manage to fly any distance from the maternal tree. We were still stuck as closely to her as ever. One of the representatives from the local authority asked Georgie a few vague questions about whether she was happy and did she get on with her foster-carer. He must have decided he couldn't detect any profound problems, or not enough to be worth uprooting her for. Or else he just didn't have any other foster mothers with vacancies available. Also, this was supposed to be Georgie's permanent, secure, and long-term placement so it might've taken a court order to get her moved on and that can take ages.

After the others had gone, Georgie and I, Sarsaparilla with Mr Churchill, were bundled into a social worker's cramped and tinny car and driven bumpily along the lanes in the direction of the dreamy tower that we used to see from the attic window. Once, it had seemed blue and mysterious. Now, it was an ordinary stone tower attached to an ordinary church in an ordinary town like any other. The only place still open was the fish and chip shop. The social worker was desperate to be rid of us. But she had to make sure we were fed. She stopped and bought us chips because we hadn't had any supper. Then we were driven to the dreariest area in the whole dreary town to be re-housed. The street had broken concrete pavements, grey concrete lamp-posts which cast a nauseous yellow light, a corner shop (closed and with a stout metal grille across the window), with a vandalized telephone box outside. There were no trees in sight, nor hedges, nor flowers, nor grass, nor birds, nor any sign of natural life.

'So how long're we staying *here*?' I asked.

'For ever and a day,' said Sarsaparilla, gently patting Georgie's head, then my shoulder. 'Till you're both grown-up and got homes of your own.'

That really *was* till kingdom come.

'Can't we go and look for another place?' I asked.

The neighbours were nosy and rude. Curtains twitched as we arrived in the social worker's car. People came to their front doors to look at us, yet not a single one came forward to say hello.

'No, Jewells, my dear,' said Sarsaparilla. 'I am not planning on moving again. I have made my bed and I must lie in it. Humbly, I admit I was mistaken in thinking to find nirvana in a rural setting.'

Was I hearing right? Was Sarsaparilla owning up to being wrong?

'I once believed,' she went on, 'that I should protect my cherubs. Remove them from life's harms. But the pathway to enlightenment is in the opposite direction. We must seek out the centre of our lives here in the spiritual impoverishment of urbanity.'

When Sarsaparilla started using long phrases you knew she was serious.

'But it's horrible here,' I said. 'It's bleak and the people are vile.'

'Heaven, my darling, is where the heart is. We shall help them to change. Seek and ye shall find. If our hearts be pure, so shall we find our little Eden here.'

She was courageous in her determination to make the most of the terrible new situation we'd found ourselves in. Even now, I admire her for her bravery.

She told us how she would, henceforward, act like a normal mother. She promised us she'd get up each morning in time to see us off to school with a cheery wave. (We were going to have to go to school every day, Georgie and I.) She'd spend all morning clearing up the house, she claimed, though I couldn't see why it'd take her all day if there was no one at home to mess it up.

'And in the afternoons I'll bake you butterfly cakes.'

'Butterfly cakes?' said Georgie. 'What's that?'

'Dear little fairy sponges with butter icing on top, like wings. Nana used to make them for you, don't you remember?'

'Your mum's dead,' I said. I felt sullen and angry though I didn't know why.

'Of course she is, petal. But that doesn't have to stop me making the cakes she used to bake.'

'All right. If you want to.'

Sarsaparilla tried so hard. She gave up collecting other people's unwantables. When we passed a skip heaped high with interesting throw-outs—cut-glass mirror, a pink lampshade, a bentwood chair, all stuff we could've used in our new home, she hardly turned her head to look. On our first day back at school, she was there on the doorstep to welcome us home. After tea (with butterfly cakes), she helped us with our homework. At a reasonable hour she sent us up to bed. She came up and read aloud to Georgie, then said goodnight prayers for each of us.

Who was she trying to impress? The social worker? Us? Herself?

She did her best to dress like a proper parent too. She quickly located the charity shop on the Lower High Street (proving she had not entirely managed to alter her shopping preferences). She bought a large beige cardigan, a large fawn checked skirt, and heavy dark tights to replace her stripy ankle socks.

I said to Georgie, 'It doesn't suit her wearing all that brown. She doesn't look like herself any more.' I preferred her flowery. I overheard two women discussing her over their garden fence.

'And have you seen her *clothes*? Gets them from the *jumble* sale!' one said.

'Looks like a bag-lady,' said the other. 'And it's my opinion, they ought never to have let her carry on the way she does. Wrong, isn't it, doing that to young children?'

It wasn't new to hear Sarsaparilla being talked about. Where we used to live, at Feeble John's, they were always gossiping. But being used to something doesn't mean you get to like it.

I hated being re-housed onto that estate. The kids called

us names. Gyppos, weirdos, hippies. At least Elizabeth wasn't around to be called mongy.

They threw stones at our windows, scrawled rude messages along our fence, pinched our milk off our doorstep, knocked over our bin so we got blamed for rubbish flowing across the pavement. They had homes of their own with cars on their concrete standing spaces, satellite dishes over their front doors, and DVDs in their front rooms so why couldn't they stay indoors and mind their own business? Were they so bored with their own lives? Did they think baiting us was more interesting?

We weren't interesting. We were a dull, diminished family, just the three of us. (Four, if you counted Mr Churchill but what's the point in counting someone who's always asleep under a heap of chewed-up newspaper?)

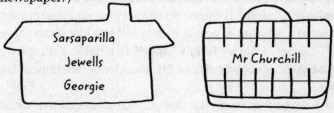

When we heard what had happened to the other three, I got depressed. Tilly was taken first to a 'place of safety'. That meant another foster home, then to meet her blood parents. They were teenagers living in a squat. Tilly's mother was the same age as Elizabeth. She didn't know how to look after her baby any better than Elizabeth would have. So she was given a nice new flat to live in and a welfare officer who came in every day to help her.

I was really peeved about that. I'd looked after Tilly for ages, without any supporting welfare officers (though Georgie had helped when she could be bothered). But after a few good nights' sleep without having to put up with Tilly's grizzling and howling, I was relieved. All babies, even darling toddlers, all pink and white and marshmallow-delicious as Tilly, take more effort than it's worth for the end result. I resolved that if I ever have children, I'll make sure I qualify for someone else such as a welfare officer to do the hard work. I'll have them back when they're old enough to help around the house.

Elizabeth's blood mother still wouldn't have her back. So she was being sent to college.

A social worker with a bulging briefcase came to inform Sarsaparilla.

'College!' I said. 'She's not going to like that. What use is college for someone who can't read or tell the time or even put her own shoes on?'

The social worker glared at me for interrupting her. She obviously wasn't used to dealing with children who had opinions of their own. She said crisply, 'The Pinnacle is no ordinary college. It offers developmental programmes for special needs young people who are all just like Lizzie.'

'Lizzie!' I said. 'Who's Lizzie? Her name's Elizabeth. And there is nobody else in the whole wide world just like her.'

Edwina was so special that she was allocated two social workers. They'd assessed her as an FTT, a failure to thrive child, concluding that she had suffered long-term emotional neglect.

I felt furious about that too. We never neglected her. It's true she was thin and weedy but if she'd failed to thrive, it was her own fault for not eating up her porridge properly. And as for those scaly red splodges on her face, which turned out to be a disgusting disease called psoriasis, it was hardly surprising they never got better, the way she kept picking at them. And if I had just occasionally bullied her and told her she was a nuisance for getting in the way, it was only because she was often so annoying.

It was quite unfair that Edwina ended up in a really jammy place, as an only child (and was probably going to turn into a spoilt only child) with a couple who had a swimming pool and ran a riding stables. They were intending to adopt her. I can't think why. But I could see it'd mean she'd get her own pony.

She was also getting speech therapy because the experts said her odd way of talking was nothing to do with having no front teeth but was a sign of her deeper troubles.

I thought, And what about me? Haven't I got deep troubles too? Why wasn't *I* having special treatment? I used to be considered so difficult that I had to be sent to the Special Inclusion Unit. Was I no longer worthy of such close scrutiny? What had happened? Had I changed? Become so well-behaved, reliable, mature that the experts didn't need to bother with me?

It was, I decided, time to stop being ignored, start being noticed. I would think up some good ways of being bad.

But then, less than a week after we'd been rehoused, something happened that changed things without me having to do anything about it. A news item appeared at the bottom of page four of the local newspaper. The headline went like this:

MIRACULOUS ESCAPE FOR FAMILY OF 6! PLUCKY FOSTER MUM, MS SARSAPARILLA GREEN, RESCUES BELOVED PET FROM HISTORIC BURNING BUILDING!

There was no mention of me by name. Nor of Elizabeth, Georgie, Edwina, or Tilly. We were just referred to as 'the tear-stained youngsters'. Yet it was astonishing what a profound effect that brief article was to have on my future life.

All thanks to Mr Churchill being saved from the fire, I too was about to be saved from my cruel life with Sarsaparilla.

Look at me now! I am no longer one of her rattletrap collectables.

How We Were Visited by a Stranger From the East

National and international events were, at the time, so dispiriting that the cheering snippet about Mr Churchill was syndicated to newspapers way beyond our local backwater. Editors throughout the gloomy globe felt that their readers deserved a mood change. The survival of a small, benign hamster, even if he had slept through his ordeal, offered a degree of optimism.

Thousands read about him. Most gave him no further thought, merely turning on to read yet more bad news about the state of the world. But one reader nearly jumped out of his seat. This could have been dangerous since he was on a Boeing 747, in club class, flying between Singapore and Osaka. He had been brought a glass of chilled orange juice, some dry roasted peanuts, and four English-language newspapers.

He recognized Sarsaparilla's name as the hamster-saver, even though the last time he'd spoken to her, he'd insisted on calling her Jane.

Stuck thirty thousand feet up in the air, when there was a lot of bad news in the world below, he was suddenly overcome with an intense feeling that he should see Jane again as a first step to understanding what life was all about. He was, in mid-air, experiencing a mid-life crisis. At least, that's how Sarsaparilla summarized it for me later, and she should know because she'd just finished having hers.

Little did the air-traveller know, while descending through thick cloud to Osaka airport, that I was to be the answer to his search for the meaning of life. Immediately on landing, he granted himself a week's leave (not impossible since he was director of his own company and could do what he liked) and booked himself on to another flight which would fly him halfway round the world to see his Jane again.

Sarsaparilla, Georgie, Mr Churchill, and I had been living in our re-housed situation for seven and a half days when he found us.

If I'd ever felt the lack of a father, Richard Browne certainly wasn't the one I was missing. What did Sarsaparilla (or Jane) ever see in him?

I saw a short, wide man with frizzy hair not unlike my own, except his was grey. His shiny suit was wide and silky. His car was wide and shiny. Georgie and I stared out of the front window, as rudely as the neighbours' kids gaped at us, as the huge car slowed to a halt outside our home.

'Perhaps she's gone and won the lottery?' Georgie said. 'And he's bringing her a cheque for fifty million pounds?'

Unlikely, as she didn't approve of gambling.

He skipped confidently up the concrete path. All the neighbours were watching too. The moment he saw Sarsaparilla, he shot his short arms out towards her.

'Why, Dickie! You old scallywag!' she said, laughing, and she put her arms out to him. Hers didn't reach round him any more than his did round her. 'You haven't changed a bit!'

'Nor have you, Jane,' he said. 'I'd have recognized you anywhere!'

'I don't know what you're here for, you old moneybags,' she said, ruffling his silvery curls in a friendly way. 'But if it's to woo me, I'm afraid you're out of luck.'

They both laughed, then waddled indoors, arm in arm, like two fat happy bears, down the narrow front hall, to the small kitchen at the back. (The front room was scattered with black bin-liners containing the half-burned items the firefighters had managed to salvage.)

Being fat was, unfortunately, the only thing Jane Green and Richard Browne had in common. And collecting things. He collected money and moved it around the globe so that it turned into more.

He brought her a load of presents. An antique warrior mask, a wind-up clockwork panda, rice-paper cakes, a miniature china tea-set, a painted fan, a wooden caddy of green tea, three coloured silk dressing-gowns.

'Kimonos, Jane,' he corrected her. He told her enticingly of his life in Japan. High speed bullet trains. Fried grasshoppers for tea. Poisonous puffer fish for supper. Rooms with paper walls. All so far away, so foreign, so romantic. Georgie and I listened, gob-smacked.

At least Sarsaparilla had the decency to be pleased with the kimonos. She slid the red one on over her shapeless secondhand cardy. It suited her better than brown acrylic.

Presents for Sarsaparilla, nothing for Georgie or me. Sarsaparilla handed the ceremonial sake drinking set over to Georgie and gave me one of the kimonos. 'This'll suit you, petal,' she said. It was blue, patterned with pink cherry blossom.

At first, he was so entranced by seeing his Jane again that he hardly noticed me. But as I put on the kimono which was too long and too wide, some memory must've jolted in his brain. Perhaps it was seeing my frizzy, straw-coloured hair.

He stared.

'Yes, that's right, you old bear,' said Sarsaparilla. 'She's our darling Jewells. The sensible one, who holds us all together.'

'Jewells?'

'Julia,' Sarsaparilla explained.

'*My* Julia? Well, blow me down with a feather!' He let out a rude guffaw like a surprised elephant. 'So it's really you, my own little Julia?'

'S'pose so,' I mumbled. I felt annoyed that he hadn't recognized me sooner, embarrassed now that he had. 'But I'm not little.'

'Just fancy that,' he said, then slumped forward, unconscious.

Was it shock? Had I done this to him? 'Is he dead?' I said.

'Course not. Just tired, poor lamb. It's jet-lag,' said Sarsaparilla. 'Long haul travel's notorious for upsetting the inner dynamics.'

Sarsaparilla, Georgie, and I dragged him over to the couch, put a folded jersey under his head, covered him with a blanket.

Later, Georgie came to my room and sat on my bed. I could tell she wanted a girl-chat. 'Aren't you a teeny-weeny bit disappointed?' she began. 'Because I definitely am.'

'What about?'

'That she's decided she can't fit him into her life-style. Did you notice, she didn't even tuck him up nicely and give him a goodnight kiss.'

'Oh, come on!' I said. 'He's an international businessman who imports rubber extruders. She'd *never* accept that kind of life.'

'But he's so sweet and gorgeous.'

'Is he?'

'And friendly. And he's not smarmy at all.' Anyone would think he was her blood father rather than mine, the way she saw all these unlikely advantages. I saw a short pushy man who was used to getting his own way.

'And look at his incredible car out there!'

'Hired,' I said.

'He must like you a lot. He brought you that fantastic silk robe thingy.'

'No, he didn't. You know perfectly well he brought all that stuff for her.' It was stupid of me to feel jealous of Sarsaparilla getting all the presents. But I did.

'It's beautiful,' Georgie said, stroking the cherry blossoms printed on the silk. I could see how much she wanted it.

'You have it then,' I said, shoving it at her. 'I couldn't care less.'

'Really? Ooh, thank you, Jewells.'

He was awake early. I heard him stumbling around in the kitchen. It was the jet-lag telling his body it was already mid-day. I went down. He was trying to find a coffee percolator.

'Or just some instant?' he said.

'She doesn't buy coffee. Just herbal tea. Peppermint or camomile and ginger.'

'Fine,' he said.

At first, even I couldn't find anything in the kitchen. Somehow, in less than a week, Sarsaparilla's daily tidying-up had managed to make it into a total mess.

I thought about what Georgie had said last night. I thought about Sarsaparilla in her brown acrylic cardigan trying to be a normal mother. I thought about the horrible neighbours gossiping. I thought about him having to witness all this muddle. I thought of being stuck in this poky emergency rehousing place for ever and a day with the kids across the way jeering at me. I thought about the social workers deciding I was all right as I was and not worth making any fuss over. I did not think for one second about Georgie or Mr Churchill.

So when he asked me his astonishingly important question, I knew at once what my answer must be.

How I Became a Daddy's Girl

'Julia, my dear,' he said. 'I can see you're a sensitive girl, and a good deal more sensible than one might expect from a child of your age. So I'm sure you're already aware that I didn't come here just to see Jane . . . er . . . Susannah.'

'Actually, Sarsaparilla.'

'Yes. Exactly. I came for another reason which I'm sure you've already guessed.' He paused just long enough for me to say 'Yes', if I *had* guessed. But I hadn't. So he quickly went on, 'And I need to ask you, would you consider coming home?'

Not in a million years would I have guessed. 'Home?' I said. 'How d'you mean?'

At that moment, Sarsaparilla came shuffling downstairs, sleepy and tousled, in her new peachy kimono. She heard him ask his question. She stopped in the doorway.

'To live with me,' he said. 'You know that you are my

only family. I've made a lot of mistakes.' Where had I heard that before? 'And now it's time I put them right before it's too late. I need to get to know you.'

I saw Sarsaparilla's face freeze, and stay frozen, as she waited to hear my answer.

'Gosh, Daddy!' I said. (I decided to try the 'daddy' thing straightaway. It sounded horrible but I persisted in the hope that I'd get used to it.) 'Wowee, yes please, Daddy. That'd be terrific, Daddy.' It didn't sound like me talking but he wasn't to know. I tried not to catch Sarsaparilla's eye.

How easily could I trade her lumpy half-cooked butterfly cakes for the experience of life in the Far East away from all this muddle? As easy as pie.

But I'd forgotten about Georgie. She was very upset. 'Away?' she said, her big brown eyes wide open as though she'd seen a ghost. 'You mean, *going* away?' She looked as though she might cry which was most uncharacteristic and would make me feel bad.

'Chin up,' I said, giving her a friendly dig in the ribs with my elbow. 'You're not the type of person who blubs.'

'You never *told* me.'

'It's my life.'

'But it's too sudden.'

'Is it? Well, I suppose it must be something hereditary. Like him.' Daddy's decision to come back and find Sarsaparilla was similarly impulsive. 'The others have gone. Now it's my turn to move on. I have to follow my destiny, don't I?' I thought that sounded important and mature.

'Have you got to follow it forever?' Georgie asked in a choked voice.

'I don't know. But for as long as it takes. Try and see it from my side. He *is* my real long-lost father. The first blood relative I've *ever* lived with, except when I was too little to remember.'

Georgie wasn't going to cry. What a relief. Instead, she muttered petulantly, 'I once lived with one of my blood parents. I had to pray all the time. It was dire. Don't say you haven't been warned.'

I said, 'It's hardly *my* fault you didn't get on with your mother. And as for Richard, well, it was *you* who pointed out he was so sweet and gorgeous. I wouldn't even have noticed if you hadn't gone on about it.'

'I said that because I think it'd be good if he stayed here with Sarsaparilla. Him and her. You and me. So we could all be a normal family together. Two parents. Two sisters.'

'Really, Georgie, sometimes you're so suburban,' I said. Why was I so stupidly blind? Why hadn't I seen that it wasn't Daddy Browne she wanted? Or Sarsaparilla. It was me she didn't want to lose. But I hadn't a clue. I was quite immature back in those days. I'm much more aware of other people's feelings now. Everybody says so.

When it was time for me to leave with my daddy, Georgie clung on to me like a jellyfish. It was quite embarrassing, especially with the neighbours watching. She tied a stupid friendship ribbon round my wrist, vowed eternal sisterhood, and told me all sorts of sentimental stuff about how much she loved me. I told her she'd always be welcome to visit me in my paper house in Osaka and eat fried grasshoppers and poisonous fish.

But she never went to Japan. More fool me. Neither did I.

Daddy later claimed he never suggested that I would.

'You'd hate it, Julia, my dear,' he says he said. 'Japanese schools are very strict. You'd never fit in.'

Instead, this is what happened:

For the first hour it was very interesting having a daddy. I got to go in his fancy hired car. For the next three hours it was moderately interesting being with him. We drove for a while, then stopped at a hotel, went to the restaurant and he told me to choose anything I wanted from the large menu card that the waiter brought. The only problem was that I didn't know what most of the things were because it was all written in French. I didn't want to end up getting frogs' legs or stuffed goose gullet that might make me throw up. But I didn't want to let Daddy know of my ignorance either. So I asked if I could have potato soup and chips. At least I knew what they'd be like.

'Is that all you want, Julia, my dear?' he said.

'Yes, thank you. I'm a vegetarian and anyway, I'm not very hungry at the moment.'

He had a huge slab of steak, nearly as big as a brick, and the same sort of colour. It was raw in the middle and oozing red. I felt quite sick watching him eat it.

Then we drove a lot longer to a commercial building where he had a meeting. I had to stay in the hired car. I played with the radio and listened to all the tapes he'd got. After two hours, a secretary brought me out a pizza still in its cardboard carton, and a fizzy drink in a plastic bottle.

Later, he took me to an educational centre. They assessed me. It was like the SIU except that he had to pay a lot of money for the assessment and I didn't have to draw any bubble charts revealing my family structure. Just as well. Some of the time, there'd only have been two names in the bubble. (Julia Daddy) Most of the time, only one: (me)

The education assessors decided that my understanding of a great many subjects, maths, history, IT, literature, had considerable holes. They advised Daddy to repair the holes before it was too late. If only they'd assessed my skill at laying and lighting a fire with sopping wet wood, or preparing a meal for seven with nothing but potatoes and half a swede, or helping a sixteen-year-old get her shoes on the right way round.

Before he went back to Osaka he bought me a trunkload of ugly uniform from a school outfitters and sent me to a boarding school. He told me, 'I was at boarding school when I was a boy. It was stonking good fun.'

I thought he meant it'd be fun like living with three hundred foster sisters only without having to cook for them. It's not. It's as restricting as ordinary day-school but relentless. Night and day. Day and night.

Luckily, because I started towards the end of a term, it was soon holiday time. Daddy came and picked me up in a different hired car and we went to stay in his London residence. It's a flat near the zoo. I can hear the lions roaring at night. Daddy says, 'You're a very imaginative child, Julia. I've never heard any lions. Nor has anyone else round here.'

To be a successful international businessperson in the rubber extruder import/export world, you have to have energy, shiny suits, determination, and no imagination at all. I'm trying really hard to get used to it.

Why Sarsaparilla Was Right All Along and Fathers Are a Waste of Space

I'm going to give up calling him 'Daddy'. Too childish. I'm having enough trouble as it is persuading him I'm not a six year old. He sends me such inappropriately infantile gifts from whatever fog-bound airport he happens to be waiting at. The other girls in the dormitory snigger every time I receive another cute china dolly.

He makes all decisions too, so I have no freedom of choice. At the start of each holiday, he returns from wherever he's been making money, picks me up from school in an ostentatiously large car, and tells me what we'll be doing. Easter, it was skiing. In the summer, he says, I will be going to a kids' holiday farm, whatever that is, then pony trekking with a youth group. Then, come September, we'll both go sailing in Greece where a colleague of his has a yacht.

When he chose the school with the yellow and mauve uniform, he hadn't counted on there being so many exeats. An exeat's like a half-term break only it's not just at half-term. You have to leave the school and go home. Only I can hardly go to the other side of the world just for a long weekend. And the progenitor can't be with me because of his overseas commitments. So I go to the apartment within sound of the roaring lions and the housekeeper takes care of me. Miss Fork has thin lips, flat hair, and cold blue hands. She wears navy-blue suits which she has tailor-made for her. My life is secure and dull. I sit by the window and look out at the red buses passing by. I watch the traffic lights changing colour. I think about wood chopping, potato peeling, washing-up in cold water and try to remind myself how glad I am that that's not my life any more, though I wish I had Elizabeth here. Her smiley face would cheer me. Maybe I'll send her a postcard of the lions at the zoo.

I've e-mailed Dadkins to ask for a rise in my Personal Allowance. I've been out with Miss Fork to buy envelopes and stamps. Now she's preparing salmon fishcakes and frozen peas for my lunch. I am about to write to Georgie. I don't know what I've got to tell her that will be of any interest to her.

I once wondered what love was. I know now. It's this, what I'm doing. It's missing some of the people you used to be with so much that your head aches. So much that you dream about them. So much that images of them flow into your brain even when you're trying not to think about them. It's about missing them so much that you'd rather hurt with thinking about them than let them fade away.

I don't actually miss Edwina, though I do think about her and hope she's happy in her new spoilt life. I don't want any of *them* to be missing *me*, not even her, and specially not Elizabeth who must be even lonelier than I am because nobody would ever want to adopt her and give her a pony of her own or take her back and give her Japanese paper origami sets. I just hope some of them want to keep in touch so I don't lose them forever. I'm writing my account of the turbulent times of rattletrap life in the back of one of Daniel's old journals so I won't ever forget any of them.

And I hope. I hope. I hope I finish growing up soon. Daddums says I should work hard and become a bi-lingual secretary and be useful in the firm.

Why must I be so desolate? Why can't I be someone else?

Miss Fork has told me her first name. Dora. I suspect she wants me to use it. I prefer not to call her anything. I don't want to grow attached. I've done with being attached to people. It hurts.

Close Relations

At school, on Sundays, pupils are allowed a visitor. Or even two. Parents arrive in their 4x4s and take their daughters out for lunch in the only hotel in town. Not Dicky the Daddy. He's always abroad moving his extruders about.

Most girls have at least one available parent, or if not, then a designated proxy. A godparent. An aunt. A grandmother. One has an elder brother who is seventeen, has a floppy fringe, and a car of his own. Some of the girls lust after him without shame.

Pops designated his housekeeper. On my first exeat she turned up in a chauffeur-driven hired car and took me to lunch in the hotel where all the other girls were lunching. But Miss Fork and I hadn't anything to talk to each other about. So I told her not to bother again.

Every afternoon, Monday to Friday, we play hockey, even I, who hates organized sport. The aim is to extinguish our excess energy, to confuse our swirling girly hormones into submission so we won't become rebellious, and cause a rumpus at night.

Then, this Thursday afternoon as we were trailing back from the pitches, the Head's secretary came out to meet me.

'You've a visitor, Julia,' she said. 'Better hurry along.'

'Visitor? You sure? I don't have visitors.'

'Yes, dear. Don't keep him waiting. He's in the main hall.'

'*He?*' Trust Dick-the-da to bend the rules and turn up on a Thursday when he knows Sunday's visitors' day. So I didn't rush. Why should I? If my old man couldn't make time to visit me except at his own convenience, then I didn't need to get myself in a sweat (any more than I already was from pounding up and down the grass after a hard leather hockey ball). I went and had a shower first. Then I slouched along to the hall.

But it wasn't Richard. It was Daniel. I didn't intend to show my astonishment so I said, 'Spot's are better, I see.'

'Hello, you,' he said.

'Hello back. You're looking healthy. How d'you get in?'

'Told them it was an emergency. Said our mother was dead.'

'Sassy. Dead?' I felt faint. The parquet wood floor lurched.

He gave me a friendly biff on the shoulder. 'Course not!'

'You lied to them then?'

'Only half a lie. *Your* mother's dead.'

'That was a long time ago. It hardly counts. And she was *my* mother, not *yours*. You shouldn't tell fibs at your age.' He'd come to see me. And all I could do was try to pick a fight. 'Well, if you're supposed to be my relative, you have to take me out. I'll get a Special Permissions exeat from the secretary's office.'

'You have to ask for *permission* to go out?'

'Yes.'

'Like prison?'

I got my exeat permission but we didn't have enough money to go for lunch at the AA-listed hotel in town. So we went and sat on the benches beside the hard tennis courts and watched some girls hitting lime-green felt balls about. The sky was heavily overcast but they were having fun pretending it was midsummer on Wimbledon Centre Court.

'Bit of all right here, isn't it?' he said.

'If you happen to appreciate sport and French.'

We sat in silence for a while, watching the balls ping backwards and forwards.

Eventually I said, 'You been to see anyone else?' I was thinking of Edwina and her ponies and her swimming pool.

'Nope. Got exams coming up, haven't I? It's seriously hard graft catching up on all the coursework. You wouldn't believe it.'

I believed it all right because he hadn't changed. Not one atom. Still on about learning as though it was the only important thing in his life. Nonetheless, he had made time in his obsessive, study-filled existence to come and see me.

'Anyway,' he said. 'I thought you'd be keeping in touch with the others. Specially Elizabeth.'

'How can I? She's in that residential place. It's miles away.'

'Yeah, but she was always your favourite, wasn't she?'

'People shouldn't have favourites, at least, not about people,' I said, all arch and prim because I knew I'd let Elizabeth down. I never even sent her that postcard of the lions. No excuse. I just forgot.

We sat in silence some more till he surprised me by saying, as though it was the most normal thing in the world, 'Bumped into Tilly in the park near school, with her mum.'

I said, 'You sure?'

'Course I'm sure. I know what Tilly looks like.'

'Yes, but how d'you know it was her mum?'

'Just guessed.'

'What's she like? Is she kind to Tilly?'

'Didn't get a chance to find out. It looked like she was taking her to the swings. So I ran over to say hello. But she must've thought I was going to accost her or mug her or something. She shoved Tilly back in the buggy and rushed off.'

'Did Tilly recognize you?'

'Not sure.'

'Why didn't you insist? Say who you were? And that you had rights?'

'Because I don't, do I? We're not really anything to each other.'

The girls on the courts went on serving each other their killer aces. They never looked over towards us, but I knew they were expecting Daniel to notice them.

He said, 'So you're all right here then?'

'How d'you mean?'

'With work and that. Like, I could help if you need it. Send you my revision notes.'

'They've put me down a year. I can manage it, more or less.'

'Well, if you do need anything—'

'Thanks.'

'I'm at Ralph's.'

'Yes. I know.'

We watched some more amazing serves and squeaky, over-the-top athletic enthusiasm. Then the sun came out.

Somehow, I prefer it when the days are dismal. When the sky is bright, watching other girls prancing about and showing-off is harder to bear.

He said, 'What about Sassy? You been in touch? Is she managing OK?'

'How should I know? I'm with my dad now. If you're so keen to find out, why don't you ask her yourself?'

'Dunno. Sometimes I just don't want to see her again. Not after the mess she made of everything. You could give me her number and I suppose I could give her a call.'

'Can't do that. She hasn't got a number.' Emergency rehousing didn't run to such luxuries. 'You'll have to write to her.'

He shrugged. 'Maybe. When my exams are over.' And I knew he wouldn't because after these exams there'd be some more.

And I felt the same about seeing her again. Not just that she'd let us down, but that we, in some indefinable way, had let *her* down.

The tennis party sauntered in for tea and prep. He didn't stay long either. Got to get back to finish his homework. He didn't actually say that. But I guessed.

Still, I was glad to have seen him. I meant to tell him I was grateful he'd made the effort. But I wasn't sure how to say it without sounding stupid. So I didn't say anything except, 'See you then.'

I felt a sick hole in my stomach watching him stride off down the school driveway. He never looked back, though I waited on the school steps to see if he would. He said he was going to hitch a lift when he reached the main road.

A tennis-player girl watched me watching him. 'Hm,' she said. 'Dishy. When you're fed up with him, don't forget to pass him on.'

'He's not a boyfriend,' I said. 'He's my cousin.' I didn't want it to get around that the relationship was closer than it was.

'Cool,' she said, winking.

The Rescue Party

Daniel's visit has unsettled me. It makes me think about the others. Just when I'm trying to forget them. I bet he only came to find me to make himself feel better, not because he wanted to know how I was.

Being emotional is against my instincts and my principles as a rational human. But, unfortunately, last night I found myself crying under the duvet. There's always a certain amount of soft snivelling in the Florence Nightingale dormitory. After Lights Out, girls start missing their pets at home, especially puppies and ponies. I must've been making quite a noise myself, sobbing for my own faraway mammalian friends, because one of the girls slunk out of her bed and crept over to comfort me.

'You missing your old man? Bet you are. I would too, if it was my daddy who was so far away. It must be awful for you. It's hundreds and thousands of miles, isn't it?'

She knows by the flowery stamps on his airmail letters where he is. There's some obsessively keen stamp-collectors in the year I've been put in where their hormones haven't started rampaging too much. They say it's for my own good. It's a year below my chronological age because of me being daft and behind with coursework, thanks to You-Know-Who.

'Yes,' I say, with misty eyes. 'Osaka's such a long way off.' But then, as I start to lie, I cheer up. 'But it's ever so beautiful once you get there. Breathtaking. With all the cherry blossom and mountains and stuff.' I know exactly what it looks like because of the hand-painted view of Mount Fuji on the paper fan Daddydums sent me last week.

Talking tourism is easier than trying to explain that the person I'm shedding tears for is my sister Elizabeth who isn't even my real sister and isn't even that far away from here, certainly not in a land of mists and cherry blossom.

I worry about her. She'll be missing me. What if the Pinnacle Residential College is as strict as boarding school and they make her do sports? What if she can't cope? What if they don't understand her? What if it's so horrible she thinks she's being punished for something she hasn't done which is something that Sarsaparilla's mum said *could* happen to you since we are all responsible for one another, for each others' sins as well as our virtues?

So before my next exeat comes round, I decide to telephone Miss Fork. I tell her I've changed my mind. I do want her to take me for a Sunday outing, after all.

'Very well,' she says crisply.

I can trust her. She's horribly efficient.

'By the way, can you drive?' I ask. 'Because there's a particular place I'd like to visit.'

'Driving is not one of my duties,' she says. 'But I can make arrangements with Mr Browne's usual firm.'

'Thanks.'

She arrives, tight-lipped, in creaseless navy suit,

upright on back seat of car with driver. Perfect. She's prepared a picnic in a wicker hamper.

I tell the driver where to go. I'm nervous and anxious. What if Elizabeth doesn't recognize me, with my short tidy hair, my polished brown shoes, and my clean cut fingernails? And what if I don't recognize her?

I'm anticipating the Pinnacle Residential Learning Centre being like an internment camp. I know Elizabeth's going to need rescuing, though I haven't yet planned how.

'Seems a well-kept place,' Miss Fork observes as we drive in through the metal gates, over the security bump and up to the main entrance. My prison has carved stone shields and mock antiquity. Elizabeth's is modern steel with grey smoked-glass panels.

We find her easily. They don't keep them locked up. She looks the same except, like me, cleaner. Her skimpy hair's washed and brushed. That's something Georgie and I never bothered about. There was always so much else to do. She's wearing it in girly bunches held with coloured clips. She flicks her head to make the bunches bounce.

She's not missing me. Nor has she forgotten who I am.

'You!' she's grinning. *'You* here! My jewel. You here, my jewel.'* She seems less double-wrapped, more confident than I remember.

'My jewel,' she says, pushing me towards a gnome-like man with crooked glasses and a crooked face, as though it's been flattened between two heavy books. He reaches out for my hand, and utters noise which I can't understand. 'Gurghn.'

'What?' I say.

He repeats it. 'Gurgn. Gurgn.'

I'm still baffled.

'John!' says Elizabeth. 'This John. John, John, John!'

The small man nods.

I am the double-wrapped social incompetent, unable to understand when someone is being introduced to me.

Others gather round. I meet Tim and Nguyen, Giorgio and Iannis, Sylvia and Nicola, and three more Johns. They all look mildly strange, as though the wind blew when they were making a funny expression. This must be how other people see my beautiful Elizabeth.

Elizabeth shows me round as though she owns the place. The others follow at a respectful distance like courtiers. She has a bedroom to herself. No sharing with sisters. Her own telly. She shows me a time-table. She studies horticulture, music, and art. She shows me the art studio. The others come too.

'Art painting,' she explains, leads me to view her own work. The others view it too, though they must have seen it before.

Her picture is big, bolder than anything Sarsaparilla ever did, and mostly red.

'What's it meant to be?'

'Not be nothing. Just fun,' she giggles. 'Painting red for fun.'

Miss Fork is unpacking the hamper. The people crowd round her like interested starlings. I draw Elizabeth aside. I have to get her on her own.

'Elizabeth. Come over here a mo. I want to ask you something important.'

She nods. Solemn. 'Yeah. Fire.'

'No, not about the fire. Though you're right, it was very serious. No, it's about now.'

'Yeah yeah. Now. Fire way.'

I realize she means, 'fire away'. Her language is advancing. 'Would you like to come in the car, over there, with me and the lady I'm with?'

She looks at me uncertainly.

'To London,' I say enticingly. 'I'll take you to the zoo. To visit the animals.'

Her bunches have stopped bouncing. She's staring into my face, trying to fathom what I'm saying.

'It's all right,' I reassure her. 'I'll look after you. Properly. So you don't have to stay here, on your own.'

What on earth makes me think that my daddio's going to be pleased to find Elizabeth installed in his perfectly finished apartment? What on earth makes me think Elizabeth doesn't understand what I'm saying?

She understands all right. She starts to chortle, her whole face brightening like a merry cherub. 'You gotto joking joking!' she says and shakes her head. 'Gotto stay here. Gotta lotta skills to do. Today, we gotto play.'

'Play?'

'Drama, play,' Elizabeth explains.

When they rehearse, I'm invited into the hall to watch. The car driver and Miss Fork come too. It seems it might be a play by Shakespeare. But not so long. Elizabeth seems to have the part of Juliet. I've never thought of my lumbering nearly-sister falling for a boy. Yet here she is, calling out with conviction, 'Romo, Romo, why you make me love you so?'

The drama teacher sits next to Miss Fork, who whispers to him.

'Oh, indeed yes,' I hear him say. 'We push these kids all right. To the absolute limits of their potential. They'll not be wanting to lie around on bean-bags for the rest of their lives, not after they've been here.'

Hey, mister! We *never* put Elizabeth on a bean-bag. She isn't a dog.

But we had protected her. She always sat and watched while Georgie and I, or Daniel and I, or Georgie and Daniel and I did the work. We let her join in games. But we never got her to help do the real things of life. She never used to have opinions. Perhaps we never allowed her to?

We can't stay. The students are getting themselves ready to go off in the mini-bus to a disco at a neighbouring college.

'Bye bye bye bye, my jewel, my girl,' says Elizabeth. 'Going to wear sparkle tonight. Sparkles in the 'air.'

'Fireworks?' I query. 'You're going to a firework display?'

'No, stupid!' she laughs. 'Ooopsy, sorry. You not stupid. Sparklies in the 'air.' She taps her bouncy bunches. She says 'air'. She means 'hair'.

Why am I so slow to follow? She's spraying glitter stuff on her bunches.

I'd never envied her before. But now, for the first time, I'm wishing I could be in with a chance of coming to a learning centre like this. Painting red canvases, going to discos, having friends, being Juliet.

I'd got it all the wrong way round. She doesn't need saving from college. She needed saving from the Greens.

On the return drive to my school, Miss Fork leans towards me and says quietly, 'Thank you, Julia, for inviting me along. That was a lovely day out.'

I don't say anything back.

'I had a sister like your Elizabeth,' Miss Fork goes on. 'In those days, of course, they didn't know what to do with them.'

I still don't reply. I don't want her to start thinking I might get attached to her. There isn't space in my life for her as well as the others I'm still attached to.

I haven't heard from Georgie. Why won't she answer my letter? Was she angry with me for deserting the sinking ashram? Does she need saving too?

On Sunday evenings, we're supposed to write letters home. I send Georgie one of the school's picture postcards. It shows off the tennis courts with a bed of scarlet tulips in front.

How I Learned Daddy Management

Guess what? Georgie's written back. Spelling's bad. Grammar's peculiar. Knowledge of setting out a letter: nil. Hand-writing: lop-sided. She didn't even put it inside an envelope, just folded over the scrap of paper (which has clearly been ripped from a school exercise book) and secured it with a piece of pink sticky plaster which is so grubby it's probably been ripped off her own wounded skin and is certainly teeming with live bacteria. Is this the first letter she's ever written?

At least she knows to put a stamp on. Sideways on the left-hand side. If her letter presentation skills are non-existent, the contents, as I read it, make my scalp tingle with excitement. First, there's the chatter.

Hi ther Jewills!!liked yr letter you sent us. What Luck you liveing near a zoo. Can we com and Visite you soon if Sassy letts me which

163

I think she will coz she is getting fed up a lot alredy with life in a orindery hom. She says she cant stand the neybors. all they do is gosip. at my school they mak us do computars allthe tim. I hate it. Im never goin to learn. Dosnt matter cos Im goin to be a artist. MR.churchil not v.well. It's the centril heatin. He cant stand it.

Then the unexpected bit. Real future plans.

We are goin trvalin quit soon If only you culd come wiv us too and be a propr family altogter. It will be a holy pilgrimage. A holy pilgrimage? What on earth is that? And how can she spell a word like 'pilgrimage' when she can't spell any of the others? She must have copied it off something. What's she copied it off? You don't find words like 'pilgrimage' just lying around. I need to know a bit more. And I need to know *now*. If only I could speak to her.

I have my mobile. Richard insisted. He thinks if you haven't got a mobile phone, it's like you haven't got a soul. And, as I know from Sarsaparilla's mum, without a soul, you're damned to eternity.

'For your own safety, Julia.'

It hasn't been much use to me so far. I haven't any friends. And even when I might make use of it for an urgent communication, it is still useless since there is no telephone of any type at the home of the person I am trying to contact.

His real purpose in forcing the mobile on me is so that he can keep tabs on me, calling me at weird times of day or night, making it seem like it's because he's in a different time-zone. He wants to know everything I'm doing. I've stopped charging it up. I've put it away in the back of the cupboard. I don't take it to school either. I don't want to go texting other girls all the way through lessons as though it was some kind of achievement. If I wish to speak to any of them (which I mostly don't) I can use my own in-built voice-box.

I'm writing another letter to Georgie. I'm marking the envelope on the outside, URGENT URGENT URGENT!!!

If Sassy has finally got the phone in, please send me the number so I can ring you. If not, here is a phone card. Here is my number. Please go to the callbox on the corner of the street just by the shop. It is my exeat extension next weekend. I will be ready every day from 2.30 p.m. till 7.30 p.m., to receive your call until I go back to prison. Love, Jewells.

I forgot to send my regards to Mr Churchill. But I expect he's OK again by now.

In the spacious white hallway, lit by the harsh steel lamps that look like aliens on stalks, of the pater's apartamento, I wait by the phone. I wait and I wait.

Then Miss Fork says she has my supper ready for me in the dining-room. If she wonders what I'm doing hovering in and out of the hallway, she probably thinks I'm waiting for a call from my dada.

I wait by the phone. I wait some more. Then the phone rings and I nearly jump out of my skin. I scramble to pick it up.

'Georgie?'

It's Richard. He's calling from Heathrow Airport. He's just touched down.

'Tell Miss Fork I'll be home in forty minutes, if the traffic's not too bad.'

His return is totally unexpected. He's terribly pleased with himself. He's brought me another doll in Japanese costume, a paper kite, and an electronic game so new that nobody in the west has yet seen it.

'I've taken extra leave,' he beams. 'I want us to enjoy real quality time together, Julia, while we can.'

He takes me to a new noodles restaurant, even though I've already had shepherd's pie and frozen peas with Miss Fork.

'Pacific and Japanese-style cuisine,' he says proudly, as though he's invented it himself. 'Don't you just love this food fusion? It's so young.'

His jollity is beginning to get on my nerves.

'You're not unwell, are you?' he asks. He's noticed I'm no longer eating.

'I'm never unwell. Illness is due to negative states of mind.'

He laughs. 'Sounds like one of crazy Jane's theories!'

I don't like the way he's laughing at her, wanting me to laugh with him.

I tell him, 'I didn't happen to feel like going out. But you insisted. I went to see Elizabeth last weekend. And this weekend I wanted to stay in for when Georgie calls.'

'Georgie?' He sounds perplexed but he knows perfectly well who she is.

'The chubby one? Dark hair? Oh. I see.' He seems baffled that I admit to preferring to stay in and talk to a girl my own age rather than going out and watching him slurp up a bowlful of wet noodles. He gazes, disgruntled, over his rounded stomach, down to his pointy-toed, polished, town shoes. He looks up hopefully. 'I haven't told you yet. I managed to get tickets for the new Hill-Billy rock-musical. I knew you'd want to see it.'

'*How* did you know?' I mutter. 'You know practically nothing about me.'

He says, 'Don't you want to go?'

I have a good idea. I put on my dear little girl expression. 'Well, I guess it'd be even more fun if my sister could come too, since she's the person I get on with best.'

But the good idea doesn't work. For some reason, it really annoys him when I mention sisters.

'They're not, are they? Any of them? You know that. The other children Jane looked after were under Care Orders. But your placement with her was entirely informal and I always retained full parental responsibility for your welfare.'

'Yes. I know all that.' Now I feel grumpy too.

'You see, Julia,' he says, as though continuing some previous conversation which I certainly can't recall us having. 'You see, Things Are Changing All The Time.'

I feel I can hear the capital letters. The words hold an ominous menace. But I don't know what the menace will be.

As soon as we get home from the noodle restaurant, Richard puts on his Kind Wise Old Father face and sits me down on the big white leather sofa beside him.

'Julia.' He says it long and slow as though it's a whole sentence in one word.

My heart sinks and my stomach rises up to meet it. I sense he's about to reveal intimate information concerning his own life which I'd rather not know about. I want to put my hands over my ears.

'Julia, there's something I have to tell you.'

My inner spirit cringes. 'OK,' I say. Cut the preamble. Get talking. Get it over with.

'You see, Julia, I've Been Seeing Someone.' He pauses so that I can take in the full significance of his words.

I think, Well, so have most people, except those who are sightless, and those kept in solitary confinement. Even I have been seeing people. Miss Fork. The uniformed doorman behind his desk downstairs.

'And it's getting serious. She's been working in our sub-office in Singapore. Now she's moved back to Osaka.' It's all coming out in a rush. I don't want to hear any of it. 'And she has a daughter, about your age.'

Dick-the-Dad can never remember how old I am. This 'about your age' could be anywhere between eight and eighteen.

'They're both over in London this week. So I've been thinking, I've been hoping, we'll experience a period of quality family time together.'

Moving too fast. Info overload. 'You're losing me,' I say. What's he mean, family time? Is he expecting a baby?

'I don't mean right away. I mean, meet up first, you and Nancy.'

'Nancy?'

'And young Jacinth. She's very like you in so many ways.'

Nobody is like me.

'And she's keen to meet you. I've told her a lot about you. Then gradually, but not too gradually, because I am getting on a bit, the four of us will make a real home together. Jacinth's at the International School in Tokyo. It might turn out to be just the place for you. We'd get to see much more of each other. I could keep an eye on you.'

Aha! So he's noticed that trying to keep tabs on me via the mobile phone is not the most reliable method.

'And I wouldn't have to do all this long-distance to-ing and fro-ing, which will be trickier in the coming months with the International Expo coming up.'

He goes on talking about his own plans. But the import/export of rubber extruders isn't one of my top topics so I get on with my own thoughts and I see two choices opening up before me, clear as a pair of floodlit pathways.

One. Stick with Dick-the-Dad, brave meeting the new stepmother, the stepsister, go and live in a luxury condominium with paper walls.

Two. Dig a hole in the ground in Regent's Park. Lie down in it. Stop living.

Quel choix. (I've started French at school.)

Then the phone in the hall rings. Miss Fork comes through. 'It's for Julia. A young lady.'

I run to the hall.

I'm squealing like a piglet into the mouthpiece. 'Georgie!'

'Jewells!' she squeals back. Nobody's called me that for ages.

'Miss you,' I say.

'Me too. I mean, I don't miss me, I miss you. We all miss you. Even Daniel.'

'Daniel?'

'He's moving back in. Didn't you know?'

'No. He never said anything.'

'He's only just decided. After he came to see us on Tuesday. I think it's Sassy's new life-plan that's turned him round.'

'What life-plan?'

'I wrote you in my letter.'

'You mean the holy pilgrimage stuff? It's a new life-plan?'

Georgie starts to tell me and I discover I don't have to lie down in a hole and die after all. There's a third choice.

Which Way to the Field of the Stars?

Georgie's excited voice goes on squealing as happy as a piglet in a truffle wood.

'So, me and Sassy'll be wearing these great pilgrims' cloaks. And these broad hats. If Sassy can find some down at Help the Aged. If not, we'll just wear ordinary clothes. But we'll definitely need some kind of hat because the sun's going to be so hot. And the nights are cold. And we'll have to carry big staves—'

'Staves?'

'You know, like strong sticks. To help us walk and to fend off the robbers. Well, that's what the pilgrims do in the pictures in Sassy's book. And begging bags. And the pilgrims each carry a cockle shell. That's the symbol of St Jacques.'

'Is it?' It used to be me explaining things to her. Now it's the other way round.

'Yes. They used their shells to scoop up drinking water from the streams and brooks. As long as you're carrying a shell, people know you're a true pilgrim so they don't mug you.'

'*Mug* you?' I gasp.

'Late at night when we're wending our way through the mountain passes. But probably nobody will because it's a bad omen to rob a pilgrim. We're not supposed to own anything and we'll be children of God. So if a mugger does decide to have a go at one of us, it'll be curtains for him. But Sassy says a holy pilgrimage is like a trial run for life so we mustn't expect an easy journey of it.'

'What's she going *for*?'

'I *told* you. To experience the simplicity of the pilgrim's way of life, and to get closer to God, of course,' says Georgie, as though everybody knows what pilgrims get up to. 'It's a religious penance for all the sins she's committed. We walk all the way, so we may get bloodied souls.'

'Bloodied souls? What's that?'

'The bottoms of our feet.'

'Oh, you mean soles?'

'That's what I said. Sassy says that's what used to happen to the saints in the olden days. The pathway was so stony it ripped their skin to shreds, specially if they went barefoot.'

'It sounds very harsh.'

'They didn't feel a thing because they were so pure and uplifted. In Sassy's book, it says if you're pilgrims, you become conscious of deeper realities of life and learn to be better people, or at least try to. She says that offering children the chance to become better people is the one worthwhile gift that a good parent can give.'

I think of all the rubbishy airport gifts that Richard sends me. Too many and every one unworthy of me.

'Hey, Georgie, what about Mr Churchill? Who'll look after him while you're away?'

'We're taking him with us.'

'A hamster can't go on a walk. He'd hate all that joggling about in his cage.'

'He's in his casket.'

'His what?'

'His ashes, they're in a little metal casket. Actually, it's Sassy's old toffee tin she used to keep her money in. But now she's got a woven purse.'

'Mr Churchill's *ashes*?'

'He's dead, Jewells. I told you how he wasn't quite himself. Well, then he died. We cremated him.'

'That's awful, that he died without me knowing.'

Georgie says, in a soothing voice, like a grown-up when you've hurt your knee, 'He was a good age, Jewells. And now he's reunited with Mrs Churchill, his earthly companion.'

I'm surprised how upset I feel.

'Sassy says we'll scatter his ashes in the Field of the Stars. It'll be so beautiful.'

'Field of the Stars?'

'That's where we're *going*, Compostella, it means Field of the Stars. You see, a thousand years ago, there was this hermit living there and he had this vision when he saw a huge bright star with a ring of little stars round it, all shining over a deserted place in the hills.'

A big star surrounded by little stars! That's Sarsaparilla, the glowing planet around which the rest of us must revolve. I know that I am one of those little stars and that I have to go with them. If only I can work out how.

I ask Georgie, 'Where d'you get the shell from?'

'Dunno. Maybe we'll collect them off the beach at Dover.'

'Dover?'

'That's where we're leaving from. Compostella's in Spain. We'll be foot passengers on the ferry. We cross the Channel, then turn right. I think it's right. Or maybe it's left.'

She's never been very sharp on her lefts and her rights. She's probably dyslexic and nobody's spotted it.

'Anyway, we turn south,' she goes on. 'Face towards the noonday sun. And we start walking. Sassy says we're not to worry about the small details of the trip, just so long as our hearts are in the right place.'

I know mine is. I can feel it opening up like a little kitchen cupboard in my chest. I feel warm brass rods of love radiating outwards to reach the whole world. Sarsaparilla's mum was right. Love is the only thing that matters.

Tippetty-tip. Tippetty-tip. The beeps. The phone-card's running out.

'So you're coming? Brill. See you Tuesday. Don't forget your sunhat.'

'Where?'

'By the ferries. We'll look out for each other.'

'What time?'

'I dunno. Middle of the day?'

'What about tickets?'

But then she's cut off.

'Georgie!' I shout into the phone. 'You still there? Can you hear me?' She can't. She's gone and it's my fault. Why am I so mean? Why didn't I send her a million pound phonecard?

I can't hear her but I can see her, coming out of the phone box outside the boarded-up corner shop. I can see her in the Elysian Fields kitchen too, nearly eleven years old, can't write, can scarcely read due to learning difficulties which nobody but loving, caring me has bothered to notice, yet managing to make half a cupful of oats go round a whole family.

She's so brave and so good and so loving. She is the best, most favourite sister I've ever had and I'm starting to cry. Tears dripping down my nose. I have to be reunited with her, walk beside her on my bloodied feet, expiate my sins at the Field of the Stars, stay with her for ever.

'Julia! Julia! They're here!' Dicko-the-daddo calls me to come out of my room. He's been twitchy all morning waiting for them to turn up.

Jacinth and Nancy.

I slip my passport, a sunhat, and a five hundred yen bank-note into my pocket. I notice Miss Fork putting scented shell soaps in the guest bathroom. It's a good omen. I paste an eager smile on my face. I skip merrily through to the sitting-room to meet the guests. 'Hello, Jacinth!' I say. 'How *do* you do. Hi there, Nancy. I'm *so* pleased to meet you.'

The mother simpers. The daughter scowls. How *could* Richard have thought we'd have anything in common? She's not a bit like me.

Miss Fork brings in a tray of coffee.

I say, 'So you two folks haven't been to Britain before? You haven't visited any of our historic sites or seen our wonderful countryside?'

They haven't. What luck.

'You know what, Daddy darling, we really ought to take them out to look at some of the sights, don't you think? Make a real family day out of it.'

Richard looks at me oddly. Is he surprised by the degree of my co-operative spirit? 'What sights?'

'The important ones of course. The ones that make Britain British. Like the Tower of London, Greenwich

Maritime, the white cliffs of Dover. We ought to get a look at them while we can before they've completely fallen into the sea. And Dover Castle. That's really fascinating. Churchill used to hide out there behind the sandbags sending secret messages to the Allied Forces.'

'Is that your *Winston* Churchill?' asks Nancy, the woman who wants to be my stepmother.

'Erm. I'm not too sure. Probably.'

'Yes, Winston Churchill, our greatest-ever statesman. A good buddy of your President Roosevelt.' Richard rubs his hands together anxiously. He's not sure what I'm up to but he's trying to help me out. Doesn't he know that I've inherited his impulsive nature?

'So if we take the lovely picnic Miss Fork's prepared for us,' I say, 'we might as well set out right away.' I add some other stuff about how I'm studying the history of World War Two at school and Dover is on the syllabus.

He's so nervous about me and this Nancy woman getting on like a house on fire he seems prepared to do anything I want. He drives us down the motorway like a man on speed. I'm relieved the cops don't stop him.

'Dover Castle, a strategic stronghold, dominates this town and harbour.' Jacinth, beside me, reads aloud from her guide book. The wicker luncheon hamper prepared by Miss Fork sits on the seat between us.

The sea is grey and menacing. Huge tankers are dragging through the heaving water. You can't see France, but you know it's not far, just there beyond the horizon.

'Stop here a moment, Daddy,' I say as we pass the entrance to the ferry terminal. 'Just for a moment. Please.'

'I thought you wanted us to have our picnic up by the castle?'

'I do.' What I mean is, I want *you* to have your picnic by the castle and *me* to say bye-bye.

'Dad,' I hiss. 'I need to go in *here.*' I nod my head towards a sign for the WC. Then I lean forward and give him a peck on the cheek. The first sign of affection I've ever offered him. My farewell gift for I am radiating with the rods of love.

Then I jump from the car. If he once loved me enough to trust me to Sarsaparilla's care, he'll have to love me enough to do it again.

Oh no! I can't believe it. Jacinth's undoing her seat-belt too. She's starting to get out. 'Hey, smart thinking, Jules,' she drawls. 'I sure could use the bathroom right now.'

A security guard strolls over to Richard's side of the car. 'Excuse me, sir. No waiting here. Restricted area. See the yellow chevrons?'

'But my daughter,' says Richard. He still thinks I need the WC.

'Just over there, sir. You'll find the short-term parking.'

Jacinth is trying to come with me. 'Get lost, can't you?' I spit in her ear. 'I'm meeting someone.'

'Someone?' My would-be sister rolls her eyes with shock and envy. 'Gee yikes! A boy?'

Her horizons are *so* limited.

'No. My real family.' I shove her back into the car, slam the door on her, and start to walk fast. Past the queuing cars. Scanning round all the time. Flash my passport. And out across the open tarmac.

I'm on the lookout for a sturdy group of pilgrims, with the remains of a dearly-loved hamster in a toffee tin.

Then, somebody's waving to me from the deck of the ferry. It's them. I can see their broad-brimmed hats, their staves, their long dark cloaks. Sarsaparilla, Georgie, Daniel. Obviously, I can't see Mr Churchill's casket, but I know it's there.

'Come *on*, Jewells!' Georgie screams down to me. 'Hurry up.'

The last of the lorries is embarking up the ramp. Crewmen are shouting departure orders. I run.

Other books by Rachel Anderson

Warlands
ISBN 0 19 275128 X

Once upon a time, quite a long time ago, in a beautiful faraway city where scarlet-flowering trees grew along wide streets, and where tropical sunsets reddened the evening skies, a small child was lying in the gutter . . .

When Amy goes to stay with her grandmother, she begs her to tell her stories about how Uncle Ho came to live with the family. Ho was a Vietnamese orphan, born amongst the bombings and terror of war, and the nightmares in his head are always with him.

No one really knew the true story of Ho's early life before he came to the family, but Amy's grandmother tells her the same stories she told Ho because, as her granny says, 'everyone needs to know the story of their life, even if it has to be invented.' And although the stories, like all good stories, start with 'Once upon a time', Amy has to wait to find out if they will end with 'And they all lived happily ever after' . . .

'A quite wonderful novel.'
The Times Educational Supplement

'Anderson's multiple viewpoint novel about the plight of refugee children is technically accomplished and profoundly moving.'
Books for Keeps

'*Warlands* is one of the most thoughtful and compelling novels for this age group I've read in ages.'
School Librarian Journal

The Scavenger's Tale
ISBN 0 19 275022 4

The taller Monitor placed her hand on my shoulder.

'You can't,' I squealed. 'My family's opted out.'

'Nobody opts out, pet. Every human being has the potential to offer the gift of life to another. Now take it easy. Just a little shot. A nice sedative.' She took the sterile wrapping off a syringe-pak while the other held me . . .

It is 2015, after the great Conflagration, and London has become a tourist site for people from all over the world, coming to visit the historic Heritage Centres. These are out of bounds to people like Bedford and his sister Dee who live in an Unapproved Temporary Dwelling and have to scavenge from skips and bins just to stay alive.

Bedford begins to notice something odd about the tourists: when they arrive in the city, they are desperately ill, but when they leave they seem to have been miraculously cured. And then the Dysfuncs start disappearing. It is only when a stranger appears, terribly injured, that Bedford begins to put two and two together . . .

'it's more skilful and interesting than any conventional dystopian horror.'

The Guardian

'One of the most powerful novels I have read this year . . . It's central strength lies in the horrible yet instructive plausibility of the future it envisages'

The Times Educational Supplement

'The most extraordinary aspect of this extraordinarily powerful novel for older readers is in its depiction of people with learning disabilities'

Books for Keeps

'A challenging, compassionate story . . . Exciting and moving'

The Express

Paper Faces
ISBN 0 19 275165 4

Winner of the Guardian Children's Fiction Award

Dot didn't want anything to change. She'd had enough of that. Change was unsettling. It meant brick dust and disorder. The war was over and she was afraid.

May, 1945. Dot ought to be happy, but she isn't. Everything is changing, she's being moved from one place to another, and nothing is the same any more. Dot has to learn to cope with death, illness, and the return of the father who is a stranger to her. She begins to discover that there are different ways of looking at historical events, different kinds of truth, and many ways of being afraid and being brave.

'Rachel Anderson has written what is in one sense an historical novel, in another a profound study of self-discovery, and by any standards a rich and deeply moving story of childhood . . . This is a very fine book indeed'
                    The Junior Bookshelf

'This is a powerful book, strong in evocation of time and place and character.'
                    The Sunday Times

'Its tough realism is funny and sad by turn, but always acutely and sharply observed . . . The depiction of war-time London is beautifully done.'
                    The Times Educational Supplement

'a perceptive, provocative story'
                    The Bookseller

The War Orphan

ISBN 0 19 275095 X

A helicopter appeared above the tree-tops of the forest.

'Attention, people of this village! You are surrounded by Republic and allied forces. Stay where you are and await instructions. Do not run away or you will be shot!'

When Ha arrives as part of Simon's family, the nightmares arrive, too. And as Simon tries to find out about Ha and his past, he begins to uncover a war-story which is not the one he wanted to hear. Is the story Simon hears in his head his own, or does it belong to this child whom his parents now say is his brother—Ha, the war orphan?

Once, Simon had thought he was in control of his life. But as the story shifts its focus between himself and Ha, he grows more and more uncertain of his own identity. He becomes obsessed by the fascination, the horror, and the all-engulfing reality of total war.

'A rare and truthful book.'
Books for Your Children

'Compelling reading! . . . A beautiful, thought-provoking story, profoundly anti-war.'
ODEC: Books to Break Barriers

'Demanding . . . a novel that stays long in the mind.'
Books for Keeps

FIFE COUNCIL LIBRARIES

FC396160

ʟᴏᴠᴇᴅ   *Sarsaperill*   *u safe*   *And I*
...d to love her back, of course I did. But being loved by someone doesn't necessarily mean you like living with them all the time and putting up with their ever-changing life plans.

Sassy's latest scheme is to pile all six of her 'collected' children, from sixteen-year-old Elizabeth to baby Tilly (not forgetting Mr Churchill the hamster), into a rattletrap camper-van and move to an isolated farmhouse so they can get in touch with their 'mind-body-spirit' and learn to be at one with Nature. This means Sassy immersing herself in creating bizarre artworks while the children are forced to practise DD (domestic democracy) and I for I (independence for infants). Jewells does her best, learning (with Daniel's help) how to build a fire, chop wood, and prepare meals for the family with nothing but potatoes and swedes, but it is not long before things start to fall apart . . .

Rachel Anderson was born in 1943 at Hampton Court. She and her husband, who teaches drama, have several grandchildren. She has worked in radio and newspaper journalism and in 1991 won the Medical Journalists' Association Award. She has written four books for adults, though now writes mostly for children. She won the Guardian Children's Fiction Award in 1992 for *Paper Faces*. When not writing she is involved with the needs and care of people who are socially and mentally challenged.